P9-AGI-892

WITHDRAWN
UTSA LIBRARIES

HERO Jesse

Lawrence Millman

St. Martin's Press, New York

LIBRARY

The University of Texas
At San Antonio

Copyright © 1982 by Lawrence Millman
For information, write: St. Martin's Press,
175 Fifth Avenue, New York, N.Y. 10010
Manufactured in the United States of America

Library of Congress Cataloging in Publication Data

Millman, Lawrence.
  Hero Jesse.

  I. Title.
PS3563.I422i4H4   813'.54   81-14582
ISBN 0-312-37004-0   AACR2

Design by Andy Carpenter

10 9 8 7 6 5 4 3 2 1

First Edition

The author wishes to express his gratitude to the Bush Foundation for its generous support during the writing of this book.

Starkly I return to stare on the ash of all I burned.
—WILFRED OWEN

"My children," said an old man to his boys, scared by a figure in the dark entry, "my children, you will never see anything worse than yourselves."
—RALPH WALDO EMERSON

PART I
Homecoming

Groundhog Day was his birthday, Venus his star, and though he was called a number of names not his own, he always answered to the call of Jesse. Call him that and he'd come running. The kids must have wanted him to run away far away from them. They called him Loony Boony and Cabbagehead or just plain Sap. Sap, Sap, here comes the Sap! They told him it was too bad he didn't have a tail. If he had a tail, then they could tie on tin cans and chase him clanking through town.

This Jesse was no dummy. He knew his own name. He knew it like he knew his old man's car: a '61 Plymouth. And now as he rested on his bed, he heard that car rattle into the drive. The front door creaked open and he heard his old man climb the steps like cannons. Boom, boom, boom, up to his room. The big cedar door was unlocked, his own door opened, and there his old man stood. Wrinkled. Bald as an old golf ball. Small. Small for a father. He got bigger and his old man only got smaller. The boy called it growing.

Jesse, go and wash your hands. Reverend's coming here for dinner.

Sold a car, dad?

His old man didn't sell cars, he only worked on them. But everyone had dreams. His old man dreamed of selling cars someday. The boy knew that and he was quick to show off.

3

His father said: Don't bait me, boy. I had a hard day. Transmissions on the blink. Carburetors. Engine valves. The works in this weather. Even had to drive all the way up Sugarhill Road because that darned Hazeltine woman got a flat and she couldn't change it herself.

Darned woman . . .

Jesse watched as his father switched on the TV. He nearly jumped with joy when he saw the war was on. His brother Jeff's war. Vietnam. Vietnam was his all-time favorite program. He'd sit on the edge of his chair watching those soldiers in action. Someday he hoped to see his own brother among them. Peering intently at the screen he'd examine the tangled jungle foliage for a glimpse of Jeff. He sought his brother in the jungles, the haythatch towns and high mountains, everywhere. Just a quick glimpse and he'd be satisfied. But all they ever showed was other soldiers, from other families. The boy figured the TV people played favorites. If he could write, he'd write them a nasty letter. *Put my brother in there you old turdknockers!* The old men who broadcast the war really ticked the boy off. They didn't seem to know about playing fair. Thought Jesse: Send those graysuits off to the glue factory.

Yet no one could cheat him of his fun. No graysuits, no one. He loved the sound of falling bombs, even better the sound of exploding ones. *Boom! Boom! Boom!* Soldiers sweeping through a town. Big double-rotor choppers, the B-52s, the Big Boy tanks, and all those nice beaches. He hated it when they ran out of bombs and the TV showed cat food.

Jesse, will you kindly wash your hands? Reverend'll be here any minute. I want you to look nice and clean for him.

All right. Do it in two shakes.

But in two shakes the boy had whisked down with the chopper into a burning town. He gazed around. Still no sign of Jeff. A person would think Jeff was better to look at than all those yowling yellow jigaboos. A brother in full battle dress, a big cidery glow on his face, and a wink to his Jesse. A brother kneeling down and with his M-60 taking careful aim at the guilty tree. And *ka-bang, ka-bang,* down like leaves fall all the gooks. It wouldn't take more than a second to kill folks that small.

Jeff did not wink from out of that bright TV screen. The boy waited. And grew. Winter blasted away summer and now winter was slowly dying into spring. Very slowly. Jesse thought about how sometimes the seasons changed and how sometimes they didn't. This last winter seemed to be going on forever. Melt and freeze, melt and freeze, that's all that ever happened nowadays in the north country. Oughter be a law against it. But at least Jeff would be home soon. Right now that was spring enough.

Boy . . .

What?

But he knew what. Reverend. A giraffe of a man of God. Long neck and crazy jiggly way of walking. The man's Adam's apple bobbed up and down in his throat like a ball trapped and trying to get out. Jesse would have liked to kick it out, too. Perhaps over some distant goalpost away far away. Then maybe the man would shut up about Concord. Talk of Concord gave the boy bad dreams and Reverend was always talking about the place.

Hurry up, Jesse. Or I'll come and wash you myself.

Concord thoughts gave way to the boy's own

face, at which he stared fondly in the mirror. And the face stared fondly back. Blond hair, a scattering of freckles, head blunt as a snake's, bright blue eyes. Bright as birdsong. It could be a TV face, he thought with some pride. And he washed it.

Reverend's here . . .

And then Reverend loped through the door, his neck all ajiggle. Jesse giggled as was his custom. The man shot him a sharp icy stare and shook his father's hand. Reverend was icy himself, his clothes smelled of winter. He said it promised snow again so he couldn't really stay too late. Janice had a cold. The kids had a cold. All in all, it was the season for colds. You scarcely needed to go out and you'd come down with one. Janice had a temperature of 102. Whatever she got, she gave to the kids. Blah blah blah, Jesse thought. When Reverend switched to colds, he couldn't be stopped with a high-powered rifle. Someone should give it a try, though.

Good news, George. The Munsons aren't going to press for a settlement. They're decent folks and they know you're not rich. They asked me to let you know that Margaret is recovering pretty well. Given the circumstances. Poor girl had quite a bad shock. Probably not out of it yet. But I saw her this afternoon and she was even smiling.

She wasn't smiling at me, observed Jesse.

Be quiet, boy. Reverend's trying to talk.

Reverend said: They're keeping her out of school for a few days. Let her take it easy, watch TV . . .

That's best. Take it easy.

Never can tell about kids. Some of them can be pretty nasty at times. Particularly at that age. They could talk to Margaret about her *new boyfriend*. Know what I mean? They might give that poor girl both barrels. . . .

Both barrels! the boy yelled. *Bammm! Bammm! Bammm!* With high-powered rifle arms he was shooting at the girl.

His old man told him he'd have to go to his room if he didn't quiet down. The old man cupped his head in his hands. Even Jesse could see he was worried. Whenever he was worried, his face would vanish behind the gate of his hands. It would get wrinkled and remind the boy of a monkey and he'd laugh. But now he put on his best manners, Jesse did. Because even if Reverend was a shithead, he was also a man of God. A person had to watch his step around men like that or he could end up in Hell. The boy clasped his hands in his lap and smiled sweetly.

Reverend: Professor Munson is going to call you up later this evening. He wants you to think about putting Jesse in some kind of institution.

That's what they all say. Get that boy out of our hair, send him to the booby hatch. No one understands. . . .

Not much to understand, George. The boy is dangerous. He had a knife. Next time he could do much worse damage. . . .

That knife was my fault. I shouldn't have let him in the kitchen by himself. Should have kept my eyes on him.

You can't watch him all the time. He needs help, George. Specialized help. I've done what I can and I know you've done all you can. But it doesn't really look like we can give him the kind of help he needs, does it?

I can give him love, Reverend. Can anyone else give him that?

Love didn't stop him from attacking Margaret, did it? Didn't stop him from trying to molest that other little girl, either.

What other girl?

Columbus Day picnic. That girl whose dress he took off. What's her name . . . Hapgood, Roberta Hapgood.

Oh, *her* . . . I'm sure that was only a game. Didn't you ever play doctor when you were a kid?

C'mon, George. I know how you feel. This can't be easy for you. Wouldn't be easy for me if he was my son. But facts are facts. The boy is not your ordinary teenager. We've been trying to treat him like he was. Now at Concord . . .

Concord? Oh Jesus!

Now let me finish, Reverend said. You know Concord as well as I do. Better. You know they're trained to look after cases like Jesse's. Old classmate of mine Ralph Pevear is there in forensics. Bright man. Trained at Mass General. I could call him up tomorrow. Ralph could take Jesse under his wing. Help him, maybe, recover. Think of how pleased you'd be if Jesse was like Jeff.

The boy's father frowned. He said: Jugged up in Concord he'd be as good as dead to me. Be just like he was dead . . .

They say it's one of the best institutions of its kind in the country. . . .

Don't care if it is. He's my son. He's all I got.

That isn't true. You've got Jeff. A son any man would be proud to have. You are proud of Jeff, aren't you, George?

Of course I'm proud of him. But does that mean I have to get rid of my other son?

I'm only trying to be helpful. Jesse's changing, getting older, stronger. You might not be this lucky next time. Know how lucky you are that Margaret's father is a professor, an open-minded man?

I'm lucky, too, declared the boy.

They turned big baffled eyes on him. Like he was some sort of strange and stagnant thing they'd found floating in their well. Let them play dumb, Jesse thought. He knew he was lucky. Not everyone had loved a girl like Margaret. He clung to that love now, screened it for himself once more.

It happened three days ago. A rare sun dozed in the sky. His old man let him out of the house and he went down to wander along the gray icespecked river. No girl body had even entered his thoughts. He'd only gone down to throw stones at dead lampreys. But then along she came in her little blue beret and a green scarf that waggled as she walked. He stepped onto the bridle path and blocked her way. A good-looking TV star of a boy such as all girls want to marry.

You're that crazy Jesse, aren't you? she asked. That's me, he replied, all politeness. The girl: Do you really eat worms? Nah, he said. Eat steak and mashed potatoes like everyone else. And for breakfast, pan-cakes with heaps and heaps of maple syrup. The girl said: Well, I wish you'd go and eat some of that stuff right now and leave me alone. He told her he wasn't hungry. He told her he wanted to play with her. Play? she said in a wobbly voice. Yeah, cowboys and In-dians . . . Silly, she told him, I'm too old for that. The girl's cheeks were like rosehips. Jesse staring at the curves of her childhood body with not a little slobber on his lips. His jaw dropping down in honest appre-ciation. She might just do for him. He ordered her to take off her clothes. Because if she was going to be a real Indian she had to be stark. Chilly as it was she had to be stark. That was the purpose of being an Indian.

She began calling him a number of names, most of them not nice, and she also started to scream. He brought out his steak knife. He had taken to carrying it around in case he found a dead animal to cut open. He liked to see what made things tick. With an engaging grin he waved the knife in front of her eyes. I'm gonna love you, he said. She screamed, You creep! Jesse: But I wanna know what it's like. Well, she told him, you just go and find out with somebody else. But I found you, he protested. It pained him that she wasn't in the right mood for it.

Nearby some dead lampreys were mired bellies up in a half-frozen gunkhole. He gazed at them, one hand clamped to the girl's wrist. He could gaze at dead lampreys all day long and on occasion he had even done so. Weird creatures, so many of them dying all at once. Their massed death haunted him. Sometimes he would cut them open but he could never figure out why they died. Perhaps the cold killed them. Kids collected them and strung their dead eyes on a hook, used them for bait. Not him. He used worms.

And he'd turned to the girl and asked her if she fished. She gave him a wild stare, her little body shaking. He guessed she didn't fish. Maybe she'd like to see his nightcrawler anyway. He unzipped his jeans and she started screaming again. Thought Jesse: Soon I'll be a grown-up.

The wheel that squeaks the loudest gets the grease, his old man always said. And with each of the girl's screams, Jesse grew more eager to give her the grease. Inside his head some lovely thing was singing for action with the same voice as those screams. He lifted her dress and she pushed it down again, pleading, Please, please leave me alone! She was crying her heart out. He knew she'd stop crying if she realized she was going to be loved.

Jesse motioned the knife across the girl's throat. He'd learned that on TV. It showed a person meant business. This girl must have seen a lot of TV. For she began to lift her dress now and with little whimpers she brought it clear to her waist. He saw what he wanted. Her little old woolly couldn't have had but ten hairs on it, a smudge of blond grass blades, springtime. Sweet fern smells filled the pores of his skin. He shoved the girl down and got on top of her. And in two shakes he was a hard pole inside her, virgin Jesse inside a girl for the first time. She screamed and he lunged and *whammm!* he dropped his bomb. He was a grown-up at last. Blood. And since he loved and admired his brother Jeff, he prayed to God that Jeff could be around the next time to share his fun.

Well, his old man said, I guess we better eat now. He tapped Jesse on the shoulder and all those Margaret thoughts settled back where they came from.

They moved to the dinner table. Soon the old man was dishing out the grub. Steak and mashed potatoes—what else? They were the boy's all-time favorites. The old man always obliged him with his all-time favorites. Jesse ate like a horse. But hungry as he was, he remembered to chew with his mouth shut. To impress Reverend. Manners are very important, his old man never tired of telling him.

Every once in a while, Reverend coughed. The boy guessed the man was coming down with a cold like the rest of his family. Send him to Concord to cure it. Jesse thanked his lucky star that he never caught colds. They always seemed to be caught by other people.

Supper's fit for a king, Jesse said.

After coffee, Reverend announced he had to be
on his way. The wind was up and it was already
snowing. He never liked driving in the snow. These
dark country roads were a hazard. If a person wasn't
careful, he could skid off and end up in a ditch.

No fun ending up in a ditch, Jesse informed him.

Reverend frowned at the boy as he shook hands
with the old man. Then he buttoned his coat. I wonder when this war will be over, he said. It was his
good-bye. Out in the darkness the snow hit the road
like grains of hard rice and belied the promise of an
early spring.

On good summery days, the kids would come
round to the house and make jokes. They'd yell up at
the boy's window, *Yoohoo Jesse,* your father tests toilet
paper and not with his nose. They'd ask him to come
out and play second base. Second base? Yeah. Just
stand there. We lost the bag. Or they'd tell him that
now that Pierre the Pisser was gone, they'd just
elected him Town Loony.

Pierre Pechee was a logger who'd lived across the
river in the Hollow. A man in a round-the-clock puk-
ing stupor. Once he'd been a seaman, but he'd been
fired for drinking the ship's compass. One night he'd
come home to find his wife with another man. You
sunnybeech! he screamed. The man scooted out of
the shack like the devil was on his tail. Then the
Pisser took a Hudson Bay axe and chopped his wife
into eleven pieces, head, arms, and legs all over the
place. One piece for each year of their marriage. The
man regretted it once he sobered up. His wife seemed
to look better when she was only one piece. However,
he couldn't put her back together again. She was like

Humpty Dumpty, only she was a woman. The Pisser was found several days later with the parts of his wife's body, playing with them like they were a jig-saw puzzle. He'd gone crazy and was sobbing away in French. The state police carried the woman out in plastic bags. The kids said her blood was dark and purple and she looked like a pizza that someone had puked up.

The boy thought this story proved beyond a doubt that Pierre was the loony one, not him. Him-self, he had never chopped a wife up. The man had even hung himself in jail. And a person could hardly follow a word he said. *Sacrémogee! You sunnybeech!* French words. Crazy as a loon.

And sometimes the kids would yell, Go bag your head. Bag it in old smelly socks. Cover your knees with rotten cheese. Cut off your arms and feed them to worms. Stick your toes up your nose. Claw out your eyes for cherry pies. Engine number nine, stick your head in turpentine. Stick it in and stick it deep, keep it there for one whole week. One Halloween they scrawled *Dodo Jesse lives here* in red paint on the side of the house. It took the old man all afternoon to scrub it off.

Teasing and all, at least the kids were company. When the boy was alone in the house, he craved that company. For the old Cape, even in daylight, gave him the shivers. And at nighttime, in his dreams, it moved. It had little centipede legs and it crawled around free of its foundations. Wherever he went, it crawled after him. Sometimes it crawled into his ears, like an earwig, and once inside it suffocated his brain. He'd awake in a cold sweat. Only a dream. But the house was as fearful as any dream. It was too old and its angles were too deep. To him old things were fear-

ful things. He couldn't really understand how they
came to be that way. They were around before he
was.

Of all old things, only his father didn't frighten
him. The little bald man loved him. Did the house
love him? Did the town of Hollinsford? Heedful
of that love he answered to his father and not his
mother, who was dead. Long ago his father told him
that this mother had gone up the chimney just as he
was coming down it. And even now despite his age he
still believed he'd been dropped down the chimney
by the stork. His mother was only a wisp of smoke, a
cloud. She had deserted him, for which he swore at
her memory. His father said she loved him but how
could she love him and then go off and die like that?
His father: Take my word for it, boy, she loved you.
And Jesse had taken that word and wrestled with it,
but he could not make it live in his bones. He figured
that his mother had died to get away from him. She
was as bad as some of the kids. She wasn't his friend.
Once when his old man took him to visit what he
thought was her grave, he gave the headstone such an
intemperate kick that he broke a toe. Then it turned
out he'd kicked his grandma's stone. His mother was
buried far away, in Concord. He hadn't listened.

His old man gave him love by way of great help-
ings of steak and potatoes. He gave him love by letting him out of the house if he promised to be a good
boy. But what he liked best was for his old man to
take him down to the cellar and show him the tools.
That's a ripsaw, there's your maul, that's a clawham-
mer, that's a drill, that a caliper, a burnisher, there's
your chisel. Your chisel will cut mountains. With the
right man behind it. Will I be the right man, dad? You

will, Jesse. You'll grow up and it'll be all right. There's your wrench. Use it to grip things.

It's fun to grip things, he'd tell his father.

Jesse, come and have a nice glass of milk.

I'm coming.

Then you go to bed.

I'm coming.

His old man had turned on the TV again. Jesse wanted to see some more war. He gaped angrily at the mouse faces of a group of child singers. Little bastards, he observed.

That's not a nice word, boy. Take it back.

Said it already. It's forever.

They're just kids. Don't ever let me hear you using that word around here again.

The boy switched to another channel. A wizened little comedian was telling jokes. Does your nose run and your feet smell? Uh-oh, you're built upside down. Motherfucker, Jesse growled. What happened to Jeff's war?

That's enough out of you, young man. No more language. You hear me? You cuss again and you're going straight to bed without your glass of milk. Understand me?

I unnerstand. No milk.

The old man: I don't cuss, don't you. . . .

I'm not a motherfucker, am I, huh? No mother . . .

And the little man could only shake his head at that, his body quivering, a mild sob in his throat. Jesse in his optimism assumed his father was talking to the TV, telling its myriad mouse faces and comedians about his son, who understood so well and who would have a cock like the President of the United States one day, a cock the size of a jackhammer. A sledgehammer. A golf club.

Don't do that, boy. It's not nice. Zip your trousers back up now.

Feels nice when it's big like this. . . .

For some reason the old man started to cry and his tears reminded the boy of the night the nasty old witch had appeared at his window and his father had taken him to his own bed. Her mouth opened wide, the old woman wanted to eat him. He yelled out in terror and his sleep-scented father was summoned by his cries. Poor little boy. You want to sleep on your old dad's arm? His old man told him it was only a dream. It was only the TV. But how can it be a dream, dad, if it was the TV? That's OK, Jesse son, you just go to sleep. But how could he sleep with his father calling to a mother he never knew? He reached up and touched his old man's tears, and his old man petted him, saying, She was too old to try it. Try what? the boy asked. Go to sleep, Jesse. You're dad's boy. Dad loves you very much. Tomorrow we'll go for a ride, we'll go to Northton tomorrow. Ride up and down the Miracle Mile in my car. See all those nice stores. I'll even buy you some kind of toy. Jesse said he wanted a rifle like the rest of the kids. All right, you'll get your rifle, only go to sleep now. With a bayonet and everything? Only if you go to sleep now. Then I will, dad. I sure will. Because I am dad's boy. And then he put his head on his father's arm and the witch left him in peace.

Will I ever have a cock the size of a golf club?

Don't.

But will I, huh, dad?

Barrrinnggg, he heard his old friend the telephone

ringing for attention. *Barrrinnggg, barrrinnggg.* His father wiped his eyes and went to answer it. The man moved slowly, like he was expecting a death.

Oh Mr. Munson. Professor Munson. Here, let me turn down the TV.

A cock like the President of the United States?

Shut up! No, not you, Professor. Jesse. Beats me where he picks up such language. . . .

A cock . . .

What's that? I can't hear you. *Jesse.* Right. Reverend told me that she's better. Listen, I can't tell you how sorry I am about all this. Feel it's my fault. I'm not much of a parent, I guess. . . .

. . . like a baseball bat. *Whammm!*

His father gave him a wham of his own. A cuff across the cheek. It didn't hurt.

Well, I know that. Everyone says that. But he's got a good home here. Everything he loves is here. His brother'll be back tomorrow. Reverend tell you about his brother? Jesse worships that boy. When Jeff comes home, we'll be back to normal again. For sure we will. Right, Professor. Been away a whole year. Fighting for his country over there. I wish you could meet him. You'd find out why I'm so proud of that boy.

Jesse watched what he took to be a baseball sailing into the bright blue sky. He'd hit that thing into orbit. The kids yelled, Home run! They jumped up and cheered him as he circled the bases, his eyes slightly wild, pride in his heart. He ran like someone was chasing him.

Yeah, I know. I know the state will foot the bill. But . . .

Crash! The boy's baserunning had toppled a chair.

Hey, let me call you back. Jesse's having some trouble. A fit or something . . .

The boy had scored the winning run by the time his father reached him and grabbed him. Stop! the old man commanded. He picked up the chair and thrust his son into it. His hands stayed on the boy's shoulders. Proud father. Proud of a son who could hit a ball like that.

Said Jesse: Cock's small again now . . .

His father gave a long shiver and the boy was concerned that the old man might be coming down with a cold like Reverend and his family. No doubt caught it this evening during Reverend's visit. He reached into his pocket and brought out his own clammy hanky, which he offered to his father.

You're killing me, his father said. Hear that? Killing me, boy. I can't live with this a day longer. Why in God's name can't you be like your brother?

The next morning Jesse woke up early and glared at the cloak of newfallen snow which covered the ground. He told this snow to go suck hind titty. It seemed not to hear him. Well, he'd make it hear him then. Old man winter needed to be taught a lesson or two. The idea of trampling occurred to the boy. He wished he could get at that snow with his flaring galoshes. He'd make it sorry it ever fell to the ground. Strong man Jesse, the one-man wrecking crew. He'd drive that snow into the earth so that all the green things of spring would have a chance. For he was a person who believed in fair play even if it only involved the seasons.

Grabbing his galoshes and lumberjack's cap, he moved toward the door. It was locked from the out-

side. He returned to the window. Then he remembered the window had been nailed shut. His dad
didn't want him climbing out on the roof. A boy was
liable to fall and break his neck. And then where
would he be? A broken neck is no fun, his old man
told him.

Trapped. He was a prisoner in his own room
again. He was tempted to put his head through the
window. He did that once before when no letter had
come from Jeff for weeks and his father said, I hope
he's not wounded or anything. The thought of a dead
Jeff pushed his head through the window. A new window was installed, made of stronger glass. Shortly
after that the letter came: Jeff was on R & R, Jap beer
stunk, and he was sorry he hadn't written sooner but
he'd lost his pen.

Jeff! The snow vanished. The boy was mindful
now that his brother was coming home today. He
hugged his pillow with a new gladness. He couldn't
wait to ask his brother about the war. It'd be like old
times, the two of them together. It'd be much better
than old times. It'd be like having a war a person
could talk to. A war of his own. Jeff, he'd ask, did you
kill many of those gooks? And the answer would
come loud and clear, like thunder: You gotta be kid-
ding me. Kill gooks? Do birds sing? Man, we sent in
mortar and blasted Charlie all the way to Kingdom
Come! Reverend can drive there and collect the
pieces. Take them in a brown paper bag to Concord.
For specialized help to glue and solder and nail them
back together again. But take it from a brother—the
stink of those gook pieces will be worse than any
stink you ever did smell. I wouldn't go anywhere near
Concord if I was you, kid. Not unless you got a

clothespin on your nose. That stink will make you throw up Jonah. Stay home with your loving family instead. Listen to a brother. . . .

I ain't going, Jeff, the boy hollered. Don't worry. I ain't going. . . .

What's that, Jesse? Where you going? his old man yelled from just outside the door.

Nowhere, Jesse said.

Click. His father unlocked the door. Porridge, boy, he said, handing his son the hot bowl. Jesse slurped with the loud animal noises he liked so well. As the porridge disappeared, he saw the picture. Always the same picture: Sleeping Beauty kissed by Prince Charming.

Why you locking that door now? Jesse asked.

I told you already.

Tell me again. . . .

So you'll be a good boy.

That's not what you said. . . .

I said I don't want a repeat of what you did to Margaret.

That's it. . . .

Later in the morning Jesse was shown the cake. It was like a wedding cake, only it was for war. A ring of candy flowers all red and yellow hugged the edge. His old man had taken a few of the boy's own soldiers and set them on top. Jesse moved them a little, so they'd be facing outwards for an attack. Silly to have them aiming their guns at each other. In certain ways, the boy was a stickler for form.

Now don't you touch, his father said. This is for your brother. You'll just have to wait till he comes home.

You make that cake all by yourself, dad?

You know I couldn't bake a cake to save my life.

Got this from Northton. The Sugar N Spice Bakery.
They made it special.

And what's it say?

Welcome Home Soldier.

The boy stared at the green candystripe letters.
He couldn't read so he stared. It was his way of read-
ing. He said: They got everything in Northton.

Northton was a town after Jesse's own heart. It
had movie houses and candlepin bowling and a place
that a person could visit and watch cattle get the hammer. It even had a police force, with flashy new squad
cars. Those cars could zoom through Northton just
like it was a drag strip. The sad thing was, they
couldn't zoom through Hollinsford. They'd be taken
out by the cracked roads and cobblestones. Beside
Northton, Hollinsford was the pits. If Jesse was a dog,
he'd wish Hollinsford was a tree.

Can we move to Northton, dad?

Jesse, I'm busy. I'm trying to get the house ready
for your brother.

Can we move to Vietnam. . . .

The boy's hometown left its imprint with the
paws of rats, with swarthy Canuck faces. And it was
only natural that the two should come together. For
the Canucks just sat around and (the kids said) stuck
their cocks into dead rats. A live rat would turn up its
nose at a Canuck, the kids said.

Dad, can we move to a place with no rats. . . .

I'm too busy now, boy. . . .

Hollinsford was rat heaven. Huge beveltoothed
rodents with brisk legs spilling out into the town from
the dump and the old abandoned mills. Most folks
had learned to live with the rats just as they had
learned to live with the Canucks. Not Jesse.

What about moving to a place with no mills. . . .

Shut up!

The mills were as bad as the rats bred in them. Jesse didn't like their many staring eyes and those redbrick faces that never smiled. They gave him the willies. There was one mill that gave him more willies than all the others. It was the one just beyond the ball field, down by the river. In its dark and moldering chambers lived the wicked witch who, from time to time, came tapping on his window. She'd eaten all the old-time mill workers. She ate anyone who strayed into the mill. And once she almost ate Jesse himself. It happened like this:

He was the ball boy, Jesse was, and they made him fetch a home run that his brother whacked through one of the mill's many broken windows. Fetch it, Jesse. Fetch it, dummy. But he'd rather just stand there, shaking with fear. Fear was better than a witch's supper. Chanted the kids: Scaredycat can't even fetch a ball no more. . . . Jeff: Show them you're brave, kid, and go down and fetch that ball. Then up spoke the town bully Raymond Perkins: Little loony here thinks some ghost will come along and grab his prick and eat it like a little hot dog. Raymond crunched his teeth down on his little finger. But Jeff stood up for him and told Raymond that his brother was no loony. The bully: Oh yeah? He's loonier'n old Pierre the Pisser and he's only just beginning. Cut him open and all you'd find is loon's eggs and *air*. . . . Jeff grabbed Raymond's shirt by the collar and shoved him against the backstop. He said: Next time you say anything against my brother, I'm going to clean the infield with your ass till it looks like raw hamburger. You get me? We're brothers and we stick together.

And Jeff had walked the boy, hand on his shoulder, right down to that mill. He kicked back the broken door. Jesse heard the rats chattering away like they were at a sewing bee. He figured the Canucks would sure like to get their hands on a few of those babies. Real live rats. Not the dead ones they got most of the time. Go on in, Jeff said. Can't. C'mon, don't shame me after I spoke up for you and everything. Jesse said he was scared, scared of the wicked witch. Jeff told him witches were only his imagination. Don't got no 'magination, Jesse replied. And then his brother squeezed his arm till it hurt. Still scared? he asked. He squeezed till a soft cry escaped the boy's feardried throat. You're gonna go in there and show those guys you're no chickenshit, hear? And he pushed. The boy smelled dead folks.

Jesse inside the old mill. He sloshed around in ooze from the river. Toadstools poking through the old floor planks. He tried to remember what his old man had said about the place. They made sleeping bags for soldiers there. To keep our boys at war warm. No, Jesse, not this war. A long-ago war. Your granddad's war. And your granddad worked in that mill, boy. Worked his fingers to the bone there. Nothing but grind, grind, grind from dawn to dusk. You can thank your lucky stars you weren't around in those days. They'd have put you to work in a mill like that one. And Jesse had thanked his lucky stars, so many of them.

Damp endless place. He moved slowly along the empty corridor. All the old cards busted up, the motors long since asleep, and galvanized pipes hung down from the high ceiling like dead tree branches. At last Jesse saw the ball in a hardened pool of oil. He took it up and wiped the muck off on his sleeves. So the kids wouldn't have to play with a dirty ball. And then he turned and headed for the door. It wasn't the door. Down the dripping corridor, across a stretch of big flat looms, no door there, either. He yelled for help and the echo of his own voice filled him with fright. And then silent he heard only his heartbeat and the occasional chirp of a rat. At first. Suddenly there came to his ears a high-pitched wailing sound. Christmas, he knew what that was! The witch! As she wailed with the voice of the wind, he hid his face in trembling hands. He didn't dare look at that awful face, wiremesh hair, warty nose. Blindly behind the cage of his hands he tripped and fell over some loose scraps of machinery. Jesse lying down in the musty dark with bleeding knuckles, hands bent to his face. The witch would get him now. He would end up in a slumgullion along with rats' tails, worms, batwings, toads, centipedes, and mountain ash. The kids said mountain ash makes a person want to expel his own eyeballs and eat them.

All the boy could do on his own behalf was cry like a baby. He couldn't speak, couldn't move, curled up in that black water. He cried like the day he was born.

That's enough, Jesse. You come on out now. The deep voice belonged to Jeff. Slowly the boy took his hands away from his face and he saw the lank form of his brother standing over him. His brother told him to stop crying but he couldn't. The witch would get them both now, two brothers together in the same stewpot. But when he told Jeff this, his brother only laughed. And when he started to say his prayers, his brother laughed still harder. My baby brother. My crazy baby brother. Bufflebrained as a clam. Jesse, you are funny. And the boy felt strong hands lifting him to his feet, strong arms taking him out into the daylight. Jeff dabbed at a bit of grime on the boy's pants and said: No such thing as witches. You just heard the wind through all those broken windows.

But Jesse was no dummy. He knew Jeff was lying, to quiet a brother's fears.

And now Jesse grew so eager at his brother's return that he posted himself at the window. Froth was summoned to his lips, pride in his breast. He couldn't wait to see his Jeff in the uniform of Bravo Company.

Hold your horses, boy. . . .

I'm holding them. . . .

No, you're not. It's liable to be a long wait. Just sit down. That's a good boy.

And his old man explained as best he could about the wait. Jeff was coming with his buddy Noley in Hack's truck. You know about Hack, son. Drinks like a fish. Pick those boys up and hit the bars first thing. Stop in every bar along the way to celebrate. Fourth of July by the time they get here . . .

Can't wait that long . . .

It won't be *that* long. It'll probably be this evening. I bet they're down in Portsmouth right now. Bars there open at the crack of dawn for the Navy Yard. Hack's got friends there. He'll want to show Noley off to them. A son that's been to war. And he'll come back here with those boys and they'll be hotter'n skunks, all of them.

Pickled.

That's right. . . .

The boy couldn't wait for those boozers to come home. He took a candy flower and chomped it. His father saw him. What did I tell you? said his old man more in weariness than in anger. That cake isn't for you.

Cake's not for me, Jesse repeated.

You just go up to your room now. Can't work and try to watch you at the same time. Yeah, go on. I'll call up to you when they get here.

Back upstairs, he went into the bathroom. He could seldom pass the bathroom without the wish to drop some black log of a turd into the toilet bowl. Those modern fixtures inspired his bowels. They seemed like a gift from God. Maybe he was making up for time lost in the cold apple knocker of his childhood. He'd go out past the garden and into the ice and chill of that shithouse. Squatting down he'd try hard but nothing would happen. His old man said he was too big for a chamber pot. Didn't want those smells in the house. So the boy always felt clogged to the ears. Fortunately the police came along. Officer Granville told his old man that it was illegal to have an outhouse without a permit. A new statute. His old man said he would crap where he darn well pleased and wasn't even a man's own property sacred anymore? Yet when faced with a fine, he installed a bathroom soon enough. That was several years ago and Officer Granville was dead now (killed in a car crash when drunk he went after a drunk) and the town of Hollinsford had been without a police officer ever since. Jesse was grateful to the police for what they had done. He was sorry they were no more.

Wiping himself he happened to peer out the window and down on the road he saw Grace Pettigrew, lunch pail in hand, heading for school. School always seemed an odd place for a girl like her. She's with the slow learners, his brother had told him. He had to ask what that meant. Slow, slow, don't you know what slow means? Turtles? the boy replied.

There was nothing slow about her now. She was no doubt late for whatever they did in school. Jesse watched her calico skirt swing above her knees, her red hair bouncing on her shoulders. She was his type, more so even than Margaret.

The girl passed out of sight and Jesse got up from the stool and with his pants still bunched at his ankles he shuffled into his own room. From his window he got a long view of her. His goggle eyes ate up her thin body. They became hands. And his hands were also hands, one hiking her skirt around her waist and the other working up a baseball bat. Then he plunged into her. Oh Jesse, she pleaded, take me away with you. Take me to Paris, France, on the other side of the rainbow.

I'll do you one better, he told her. I'll take you to Vietnam.

Vietnam . . .

Nam's where I'm headed, with my brother and his buddies. It's the greatest! You can sun yourself on the beach while we go after those gooks. Else they'll come over here and fuck everybody's mother and eat everybody's dog. Brother wrote a letter about them eating dogs.

Can I wear my bikini?

Love it!

And off they went, flying through the air with the greatest of ease, a guy and his gal on their flying trapeze.

After Grace, the boy lay down and the sandman paid him a visit. He napped for he knew not how long. He awoke to his brother crashing across the room as though he was on a destroy mission. Jeff! The boy expected to be hugged and kissed and told how big he'd grown. Instead Jeff proceeded to clobber him. His brother wasn't playing around. A rocklike fist rammed into Jesse's gut. A hand smacked his ear and he heard a whooshing sound deep inside his own head.

Cut it out, Jesse said. It's me. Your brother. Ain't no gook. Can't you see I'm your brother? The guy who you grew up with?

You're no brother to me! Jeff hollered.

Savage hands, beery breath. Jeff was plastered. How else explain his forgetfulness? Drink made a person think he was back in Vietnam even after he'd come home.

Stop! Jesse cried. Gooks got slanty eyes. Eat rice. I don't never eat rice.

But Jeff went on torpedoing away. Right, left, right. The boy's nose was bleeding. Blood tasting like iron. Open fists, closed fists, rocks against his ribs. Finally Jeff stopped and just stood over him, breathing heavily. Why'd you do it, Jesse? he said. Why'd you rape that little girl? She didn't do you no harm. Can't you answer me? I'm away for a year and I come back and my brother's a fucken pervert.

Jesse said he only wanted to be a grown-up. He knew it was right around the bend, but he just couldn't wait. He was an eager boy.

Grown-up, my ass! You about broke your dad's heart. Know that? You're not a grown-up by raping little girls. That's just perverted. Like Sam Pettigrew.

Sam's older, the boy protested. At this his brother could only throw up his arms and storm out of the room. Aching and confused Jesse didn't know whether he'd given the right answer or not. He got down on his knees beside his bed and begged God the Almighty to please make his brother friends with him again, friends like they'd been before Jeff left for his war.

He was still on his knees when he heard Hack Newton's gravelly voice. Come and get it, Jesse boy. Soup's on.

His face felt like a John Deere had run back and forth over it. His temple throbbed in the direction of his eyes. He touched his nostrils and his thumb cracked away small amounts of blood. He probed his tongue inside his lip and the flesh seemed miles away. His ribs twinged, they wanted out. He walked stiffly down the stairs, meeting Hack at the bottom. The pot-bellied trucker leered at him. Sorry t'disappoint you, the man declared, but we got no pussy on the menu tonight. Just hot dogs and Vietnam cake. Less you want us to dig up a doughnut for you. One with a real ... big ... hole. A real *grown-up* doughnut. The man tittered like a demented schoolgirl.

I'll take the doughnut, the boy said. He edged over to his brother, who sat with his buddy Noley, beer cans in hand, looking at the TV. Jesse watched as a war party of Indians whooped down from the hills on their ponies and torched a farmer's home and tomahawked his pigs, likewise his wife and kids. Ain't they ever heard of cars? the boy wondered. The Indian chief cleaved the farmer's scalp all shaggy and bleeding from the man's head.

How's tricks, Jesse? Noley said.

Fine.

Jeff was silent, his mouth clamped shut like a turtle's, and on his own face a grim determined frown. Kill any of those gooks, Jeff? the boy ventured cautiously. His brother sipped from his beer and ignored him. Jesse waited. The Indians hit another farmstead. And he headed for the kitchen.

A great hardwood fire blazed away in the wood-stove. His old man had done his best to brighten things up. Red and orange crepe paper hung on the chairs and table. Tacked up on the wall was an old poster of Uncle Sam bayonetting a trio of Japs like they were morsels of food on a skewer. Jesse couldn't read the caption, but he knew it was nice. Like Jeff's coming-home cake was nice. There it was, in the middle of the table, girded by the glitter and gold of Christmas ornaments. No doubt the old man couldn't locate any Vietnam ornaments in time. But that was all right. It was clever to think of Christmas ornaments. Jesse did not feel angels were at all inappropriate to the soldiers rising out of the top of the cake.

This cake made his face feel better. He noticed a few slices had already been taken so he tried slicing a piece of his own. He produced only a pile of crumbs. But he grabbed those crumbs, nothing wrong with crumbs, and shoveled them into his mouth. Another mouthful of crumbs followed. He took care not to eat a soldier.

By now the boy was starved fit to eat the Lord's Supper. He snatched potato chips and heaps of popcorn. He snatched a pickle. Chewing everything together with the cake he could almost imagine himself at a picnic. He only missed his friend the great out-of-doors.

All that popcorn put him in mind of the church picnic and Roberta Hapgood. He had only wanted to see what was under her bright blue skirt. I'll give you some popcorn, he said. Okeydokey, she told him. But first you'll have to take off your skirt and undies. Okeydokey. She removed them and he gaped at her tiny seashell. He hadn't seen one of them ever before. It looked like it had been beaten and beaten again by someone's fist. It wasn't much, but he had to start somewhere. Trying to understand this thing called love. If he could, he would have taken notes. Instead he gaped—that was his way of taking notes. Sometime later they found him with the same implacable look on his face. And the little girl half-naked and munching popcorn. They could berate him all they wanted, box his ears and send him home, he had only looked. Looked, not touched. This girl was too young to touch.

Hack brought him back. Bet your dad's chow don't taste as good as poontang, said the trucker. From whom a noisome reek of beer spread in all directions. Jesse turned away. He did not care for the man at all.

From over by the stove his old man said: Leave the boy alone, Hack. He's been waiting all day for this.

Hell, George. I was only going to talk politics with him. Anything wrong with that? I was only going to tell him he should be proud to be living in a country where the women got class. You take those Vietnam girls that Noley was telling us about. They squat and piss right there in front of you on the sidewalks. I mean, they don't even know the meaning of a toilet. Got no education, nothing. Hell, if Gladys did something like that I'd dropkick her halfway to Boston.

I do believe you would.

Course I would. I don't take to crudity at all.

You're drunk, Hack. Why don't you lie down for a while? You'll feel better.

We all been lying down for too long. That's what I say. I say, Go over there and A-bomb those fucken yellow fucks. A load of A-bombs'll speak louder than what we been doing. We got to stop acting like an old sow that's not got enough strength to keep the kink in her tail. The trucker put a finger in his mouth to adjust his teeth. Or this damned war'll go on forever, he added softly. And flipped open another beer.

His father was cooking hot dogs and to the boy that seemed to speak louder than all of Hack's politics. He moved to the stove and put his arm around the little man, who ran a quick inspection of the boy's bruised face, the rind of blood under his nose, and then returned to the hot dogs. The sight of the battle-worn Jesse seemed to weary him. With his back to his son he said: You oughter let me put a Band-Aid above that eye. It looks ugly.

It doesn't hurt no more.

Then you haven't felt it yet. Wait till tomorrow.

Felt it fine. Jeff was only playing.

Don't need to play like that, boy. No one does. But your brother's sorry for what he done. I know. He's just dogtired. Hasn't slept in two nights. Let him get a good night's sleep and he'll be good as new. Then you and him can go to Northton and ride up and down the Miracle Mile. Sound OK?

Jesse nodded.

We should be thankful he's home safe and sound, the old man said. A lot of brothers come back home in a casket with a flag draped over them.

Fun. Can I get a casket, dad? With a real American flag?

Jesse, you don't have any idea what a casket is. A casket is the same as a coffin.

Well, I'll just take the flag then. And the boy saw himself draped in the flag, minus a casket, coming home from war. He saw himself strutting in front of the kids like the cock of the walk, and none of them would dare call him crazy for fear of insulting the American flag. That's Hero Jesse, they'd whisper. Home on leave from winning the war. He's real *scenery*, man. Bet even his underpants are made of flag.

Jesse went back to his brother. He'd tell Jeff he understood. Can't be awake for too long or you'll begin to do strange things. Like beat up on your Jesse. But the boy forgave his brother. Tomorrow they'd set out in Jeff's souped-up Dodge and hit Northton and once again as in the old days the town would prick up its ears when the two hellraisers came roaring through. Once again they'd be best friends, and forever after.

But both his brother and Noley were fast asleep. Jeff's jaw sagged open and his mouth was an open cavern of beer smell. Noley in his sleep was mumbling sweet nothings to the TV. Poor bastards, thought the boy. All that war, it takes something out of a man. He laid a gentle hand on his brother's shoulder and whispered into Jeff's ear, Tomorrow we'll hit Northton and burn some rubber and have a pizza.

Jesse, got just the girl for you. Tits like a bitch. Only trouble is, she is a bitch. Labrador retriever, hahaha . . .

The boy brushed past Hack and at the icebox took his milk and drank from the bottle. His old man let him drink from the bottle because no one else in the family drank milk. This way he'd only get his own germs. And he had none.

Hack seemed to have latched on to him. The trucker said: Have a beer, boy. Beer'll put hair on your chest. And he opened his shirt to display what Jesse considered a very sparse growth of hair; hair that was gray and stunted and hardly worthy of the name. He dared not say so. Instead he said: Milk makes a person strong.

Baby's drink . . .

His old man said: Give the boy a break, Hack. He's too young to drink.

Only trying to educate him, George. Only thinking of his future. You don't want him to grow up and
be a milkguzzling queer, do you?

Maybe I just don't want him to grow up and be a
drunk. Maybe he'll grow up and believe in some
other God than a six-pack.

Ain't no other God. Least to my knowledge.

That's about as funny as a heart attack, Hack.

For a minute or so the trucker looked like he was
trying to figure out what was so funny about a heart
attack. He frowned, rubbed his chin. And he seemed
to be a little more sober. He said: George, you hear
about Horace Garr's girl Marylou? Ponytail got
caught in her old man's thresher and her face got
pulled clean off. Just like you was pulling off a mask.
They got her down at the Hitchcock now. Grafted her
lips and eyelids and everything to her belly till they
could give her a new face. Can you believe that?
Heard it down at the Cartier Club the other day. . . .

Doctors can do just about anything nowadays,
the old man observed.

They sure can. And then turning to Jesse the
trucker laughed and said: Bet you'd like to graft
something to her belly, eh, chum! He gave the boy a
slap on the back that sent prickles running raggedly
across his skin. Quivering with an obscure anger Jesse
looked to his father, to see would the old man bash
Hack for hitting his son. Knee him in the balls and
wipe the hardwood floor with his ass. But his father
couldn't seem to tell anyone to pump sand these days.
Weak as a baby. Too old. Too bald. One foot in the
grave and the other foot running to join it. The only
cannons in him were those feet and that was only
because the house was old and turned every sound
into one cannon or another. Thought the boy: Dad's

time is over and done with. Soon I'll have to be strong for him.

The old man threw one last hickory log into the woodstove and yawned. A yawn like a drawnout moan. He said to Hack: Isn't it time you and Noley thought about going home? It's getting late and everybody's bushed. And with that he collapsed into his Boston rocker, saying, It's been a long day for all of us, and in a few seconds he was asleep himself, snoring loudly. His snores sounded to Jesse like he was gasping for air, like death had pitched its tent in his throat. Back and forth, back and forth, the chair rocked, carried by its first momentum, till it likewise came to a halt.

Sweet dreams and thanks for the memory, Hack said. Instead of leaving he lurched to the icebox and brought out two more beers. He offered one to the boy. Again Jesse refused. Milk was his drink and always would be. He knew what alcohol did to a person's brain. Ate away at it like acid. Till you got a man like Pierre the Pisser, who went crazy and hung himself.

You can have that slop, Jesse said.

All right, be a queer if you want to. I don't care.

And you—you're going to hang yourself, the boy thought. By the neck until dead. In his mind he programmed a scene of Hack at the end of a noose, the burly body swinging awkwardly, eyes popping and the fat tongue bulged out. Satisfied by that, Jesse stuffed a crumbly handful of cake into his mouth.

Hack at the TV paused to say horseshit to a Tarzan movie. Then rapidly switching channels, traveling the knob twice and three times over, he said horseshit to it all, now to a talk-show host, now a deodorant pad, It's all horseshit and it won't flush.

Too late for the war, Jesse informed him. He hoped the man would now go home.

But the trucker only nodded and said to him: You're right there, kid. Hundred percent fucken right. We oughter go in there and blow the whole country off the fucken map. And get a few of those Rooshkies while we're at it. Dump one of them big warheads on the Kremlin. Got the weapons, we should use 'em.

The boy didn't like Hack butting in on his war. Let the man go find a war of his own. Jesse had his own. Bravely he told the trucker: Keep your mittens off my war. . . .

Me? Never touched you, boy. You're the fruit-cake around here, not me. Just say I touched you once more and you're gonna get your face cracked like you never got it cracked before.

And in Jesse's head the enemy trucker swung from a noose tied to a chopper's propeller and even the gooks in their rice paddies had to grin as overhead Hack passed like he was on a crazy merry-go-round.

You're on a merry crazy-go-round, the boy shouted. In his anger getting the words a little mixed up.

C'mon Jesse have a beer and let's be friends. . . . The man put a limp heavy arm around the boy's shoulders. Uncle Hack knows you're no queer. You're like your Uncle, a first-class pussy hound. And he let out a long and rather mournful beagle howl. *Aww-rooooooo!* Another stale billow of beer enclosed Jesse, who backed away.

You go home, the boy said.

But Hack's bull face again pressed close to him, so close that he could just about see each one of the thousand red spiderwebs drawn to the tip of the man's nose. The mouth opened slowly. I'm a pussy hound, too. . . . It opened wider and wider, Jesse didn't know whether it was going to swallow him (another Jonah!) or only speak. It spoke. Tell me what was it like with such a little . . .

Already the boy had grabbed the half-full milk bottle and brought it whishing through the air with all his might. Holding the neck end he aimed it toward the man's mouth, or what would have been his mouth if Hack hadn't ducked. The bottle hit him squarely on the side of the head and with a *thunk!* neatly broke into two halves, splattering milk across the floor. Hack dropped like the bones in his body had turned to liquid, a wallow of flesh crumpling onto the table and off it and onto the floor. A thin trickle of blood started seeping out of his nose, an even thinner trickle from his mouth. One of his eyes was open and one half-shut. On the trucker's face was a look of mild surprise.

Now are you going home? the boy asked.

No answer. Jesse regarded his handiwork. Hack had no breath except beeriness. No fucken this or fucken that on his lips. He didn't move. The man looked exactly like dead people looked on TV. And then it dawned on the boy that Hack must be dead. He wondered if that was the last of the milk. He went to the icebox to check. It was.

And so he had a dead trucker on his hands. The boy hadn't really meant to kill Hack, only stun him and by stunning him let it be known that the man was no longer a welcome guest in the Boone house. It was Hack's own fault he had gotten in the way. Put his dumb head where his mouth should have been. Said Jesse to the man: Dummy . . .

He inspected the body for more blood. He

searched hard but there were only a few little trickles here and there. Why wasn't Hack more bloody? Eben Taylor was one other man who didn't seem to have much blood. He'd fallen down dead as he cleared brush from his back forty. His nephew Raymond Perkins said he looked like he was only asleep, cradled there in the sumac with no blood, nothing. But Eben Taylor was nearly eighty and a person couldn't expect a man that old to have much if any blood. For the boy thought blood went away with the years. It was happening to his own father before his very eyes.

He rolled Hack over. No blood on his backside, either. The boy was puzzled. The trucker hadn't been on the downhill side of life. But maybe the blow had gone straight to his brain and silenced it before it could direct the blood to run. Or maybe drunks just didn't have much blood. They had beer where blood should be. If so, why wasn't beer dripping from Hack's nose? He still had so much to learn about the body's workings. Answers he couldn't get by cutting open dead lampreys.

Gore or no gore, the killing had been easy. Killing Hack was one of the easiest jobs he'd ever done. Far easier than tying his shoelaces in the morning. Gazing down on the trucker he felt a keen sense of pride.

Jesse had seen enough TV to know that he had to get rid of the body. It struck him that they'd blame his brother for the murder. A soldier home on leave, afraid he'd get out of practice. The soldier gets itchy and he happens to knock off one of the hometown folks. Coldblooded murder, they'd call it. And ship poor Jeff out to death-row and starve him on hardtack and water. When he was no more than skin and bones, they'd make him face a firing squad of his own buddies. Dishonorable discharge. You'd just love that to happen, wouldn't you? Jesse said to Hack. And he trembled at what lay in store for his brother. He had to save Jeff. Because brothers stick together like glue.

He pulled at the nape of Hack's shirt till the material parted in his hands. He grabbed a leg, a fleshy paw. The body had a mind of its own. Jesse swore and wished he'd killed a smaller man. Then he remembered the way they did it on TV. He took the trucker under arms still wet with sweat (did dead people sweat?). Hack sprawled heavily, his head lolling, and with a little coaxing—Get a move on you dead cocksucker you!—the man began to move. Jesse dragged him across the floor.

The sleepers weren't roused by any of this noise. They remained only slightly less dead to the world than Hack. The boy could have dropped a safe on their heads and they wouldn't have uttered a peep. Except in their dreams.

Finally he got his load to the door. Crystal stars greeted him, and the night. His breath exploded in the outside cold. Spring, he snickered. Supposed to be spring and all we got is more winter. He yearned for Vietnam. Where spring was spring and no fooling around. He yearned to bury himself in warm jungle and sweet birdsong such as this barren north country would never know. He kicked the ground, which was snow.

He returned from the garage with a gunnysack and pulled it over the body. Then he heaved with all his strength, lifting and folding Hack into his red wagon. Friday was dump day. His idea: to drop Hack off at the dump.

Toting the garbage in his wagon was the one task

that his old man ever asked of him. The boy per-
formed this task once a week. Sam Pettigrew was so
accustomed to seeing him at the dump, he would as-
sume the load was just more garbage. As, in a way, it
was. Once in the pit Hack would burn like a piece of
dry winter wood. He would burn right down to a
handful of gray ashes identical to the ashes of old
newspapers, mattresses, and dead pets. Next day his
father would ask him what became of Hack and he'd
smile and say, Why Hack just went to take a dump.
It'd be a miracle if he could keep from laughing.

The wagon creaked on its iron wheels, stubborn
at first. Soon it gathered a motion despite the thick
slush. A person could haul anything with this wagon.
Sam Pettigrew said so himself. Sam said it would outlast all of them. All of who? You, me, your dad, all of
us. Iron and metal, they'll be around when we're feeding the worms. Sam often said silly things like that.
As if the boy would ever bother about feeding worms!
But he liked the dumpkeeper nonetheless. How could
he not like a man who was both father and grandfather to the same girl? That was Sam's claim to fame.
Otis Dimick the stonemason's son told the boy the
whole story:

One night Sam came home worn and weary from
his job at the broom-handle factory. He tumbled into
the first bed in sight, his daughter Lucy's. Lucy happened to be in it at the time. Soon he was cuddling
the girl in his arms. Did he mistake her for his wife?
Did she try to fight him off? No one in town knew for
sure, though they had their ideas. In a little over eight
months his daughter gave birth to Grace (stork
dropped her down the chimney, Jesse corrected Otis.
Later he thought this birth a marvel, for the Pettigrew
trailer had no chimney.). And not long after that Lucy

and her mother went away to California, leaving Sam
to look after the little girl. The man dropped out of
work so he could care for Grace. Soon he was on the
rolls of the town poor and like everyone else on the
poor rolls at one time or another he was given
the dump to attend. Moved his trailer there, and his
daughter. He said they'd take Grace away from him
over his dead body. By *they* he meant the law. But the
law seemed to have no need for the girl. Maybe, Otis
said, because she was a little soft in the head. If her
head is soft, Jesse thought, then so's mine. Soft as a
rock. Break windows with it . . .

The wagon hit a bump and Hack nearly tumbled
out of his gunnysack. Trying to get away, eh? Jesse
said to the trucker. He trussed up the sack so the dead
man couldn't escape.

Each step toward the dump took him closer to
Grace. He began to think about the girl. He knew she
was similar to him as no one else in Hollinsford was
similar to him. Her eyes told him, and her smile.
Whenever she said Hello or It's cold, he knew.
Though exactly how they were like each other he
could no more say than he could say why the lampreys died.

Freckled face, flowing red hair, slender girlbody.
A late-night visit was on Jesse's mind. He approached
the gate with some eagerness. His wagon felt light, its
cargo like a sack of goosedown. The road over which
he now pulled Hack was packed with cans mashed
flat and sprinkled with broken glass. Folks got flat
tires from it all the time. Never Jesse, never his
wagon.

He raised the latch and entered the dump.
Ruined cars and John Deeres lay like the victims of
some long-lost holocaust, upturned and skeletal,

picked over for all they were worth by Sam Pettigrew.
Sam had set out tables and chairs for people who
furnished their houses from the dump. Through the
trees Jesse could see the blue-scarlet smoke of scattered fires. His nose scented the old tires that Sam
used to keep everything ablaze. He could hear the
rats, thousands of them, creeping over great levees of
garbage, evil creatures who slept by day and came out
in the darkness. Raymond Perkins said they were
what glue was made from, and bubble gum.

Jesse didn't usually visit the dump this late. He'd
learned his lesson. That lesson came from a time that
now seemed like a different place. He'd been enjoying
the smells of things burning and he'd lingered too
long after dark and he was set upon by a huge de-
ranged rat the size of a dog. It must have mistaken
him for a morsel of decayed food. The rat treed him.
Its eyes were orange and fiery. Scram, go away, he
told it. Get away from me. I'm Jesse. A boy. Rats don't
eat boys, they eat shit. Why don't you just go on
home and eat a nice supper of shit? The rat held its
ground. Then two of Jeff's friends showed up for a
little target practice in the half-light of burning garbage. Chuckling they pointed to Jesse up in the tree
and called him a loony. The boy hollered: Take it
away, take it away. At last one of them shot the rat
through its sleek head and shot it again through the
stomach when it lay dead and its guts spilled out all
putty-colored. They put a cherry bomb in the rat's
mouth and blew its head loose. A little piece of jaw
sailed past Jesse. They shot the animal again and
again till it was hardly more than a scrap of raw gore.
Loony! they shouted up at the still trembling boy and
walked off.

But now Jesse moved among the rats like he

owned the place. He'd grown up a lot since his run-in
with that huge rat and he'd also killed Hack. He knew
they could sense this because not one rat deserted its
garbage for him.

He picked his way through an everlasting maze
of battered iceboxes and washers and old mattress
springs, all indifferent to flame. He came to the bank
below which the fires smoldered. The smell was not
unpleasant. He asked the Almighty to look after
Hack's soul and he yelled *Bombs Away!* and tipped his
wagon and down into the pit rolled Hack, landing
among charred bean cans and metal shards. Right
away the sack began to smolder. Soon it would be
burning and the trucker burning with it. The boy
knew his Jeff was safe now. The law couldn't touch
him. He could go back to Vietnam instead of to death
row.

Jesse stood at the door of the Pettigrew trailer, his
knuckles clacking against the corrugated metal. Beside the cinder-block steps was a pile of hubcaps
stamped with kingly crests. Medallions looted from
the garbage.

From the crack in the door Sam's eyes narrowed
on him. Jesse . . . and what are you doing here this
time of night? The man opened the door a little wider.

Jesse pointed to the beer can in the dumpkeeper's hand. Will outlast us all, he said. He stood
there as though that was enough of a message. He
wanted to get on Sam's good side. His child's grin
scurried across the bottom of his face. He moved back
a few steps to prove that it was only him, not some
night-visiting monster.

What *do* you want, kid? I don't got all night.

The boy could hear a Tarzan yell on the TV inside the trailer, and he heard the jungle answer that yell with a welter of animal screams. I want to see Grace, he said at last. He mounted the steps again but Sam held out the stop sign.

Rape her, don't you mean? Boy, I don't know what's come over you. Gone crazy with the long winter or what. But I do know you're not going to lay a finger on my daughter. Grace's all I got. I'd kill you if you went after her like you did that Munson girl.

He hadn't expected this rebuke. Nor had he come for talk of killing. He could get that at home—in spades. He blurted out: You're too old to be screwing her. . . .

Why you little sonafabitch. The dumpkeeper's voice quivered with anger. You oughter be horse-whipped for saying something like that. Now you get home before I call up your dad.

Grace's angel face appeared behind her father. Nice big deereyes. Hi, Jesse said. It was all he could think of to say just then. Sometimes he was shy around girls.

Elefunks stampeding on the TV, the girl announced.

Keep away from him. He's up to no good. Her father brushed her back, spilling his beer. Shit now look what you made me do. Get the hell home, boy. Or I'll really lose my temper with you.

Oh let him watch the elefunks, papa. . . .

I wanna see the elefunks, Jesse said.

Then get on home and watch them on your own TV. It's got them the same as ours.

Oh papa. Kindly let Jesse watch. Tarzan and them'll be over and done with on his TV.

Kindly let me watch, Jesse mimicked Grace's voice, trying to win the man over. But Sam seemed put out rather than won over. He shoved the boy down the steps and slammed the door, and Jesse landed on the hubcaps, which collapsed, rattling and rolling.

He didn't get it. The dumpkeeper had always been his friend. They'd sit and shoot the shit, Sam pointing to some half-charred lump of trash, some contorted metal skeleton or household appliance, and ask Jesse could he identify it. The boy seldom could. Why that's an icebox! Sam would declare. See that thingum, that's a wheelchair! Fun game. And unlike the other kids Jesse never chanted, Sam, Sam, the old dump man, screwed his daughter and away she ran. He figured Sam might not play the garbage game if he went around reciting that rhyme.

Perhaps the man was just worn out. He wanted his beer and to hell with everything else. Friday was a long day at the dump. Most of his customers came on Friday. Sam had to be up at the crack of dawn and bulldoze all that debris and light fires till dusk. The boy could sympathize with that. And he would sympathize with it. Up he got and knocked on the door again. I'm back, he hollered. This time Sam appeared at the door armed with the .22 that he used to shoot rats. Poor bastard, Jesse sputtered. His sympathy. The dumpkeeper blasted a hole in a ragged mattress only ten or so feet away. A few chicken feathers fluttered up and softly fluttered down again.

At that the boy beat a hasty retreat. He respected guns. They spoke mightier than words.

And don't come back, Sam called after him.

I'll be back, Jesse gasped between breaths. He had to come back, what with the Pettigrew trailer struck by a mortar round (would those gooks never give up?) and pulsing with flame, hot yellow flames

gaggling everywhere, and poor Grace yelling, Save
me, save me, oh please won't somebody save me? He
saved her, did Hero Jesse. He heard her cries from
afar and came running. He fought the flame though it
singed his hair and fought the smoke and he carried
Grace from the burning trailer swathed in sheets and
blankets. Inside them she was naked. Christmas! A
pink-skinned grateful girl. Take me with you, Jesse.
To Vietnam at the end of the rainbow. I wanna be
yours forever and ever. He told her all right. Unfortu-
nately Sam the dump man was burned to a crisp by
the time the boy returned to rescue him. Those gooks!

Jesse went to the pit where Hack lay smoldering.
The dump was doing its job well. He sniffed, savoring
the scent of french-fried trucker. And then taking the
tongue of his wagon he started toward home. He
passed not a soul along the way. He guessed it was
past most folks' bedtimes. Only a ghost or some night
monster would be up at this hour.

He got home to find Hack's truck still parked in
front of the house. That came as no surprise to him.
He had never known a truck to drive off by itself.
Inside the house no one seemed to have moved an
inch since he left. They slept on, a chorus of snores
and wheezes. They slept like they hadn't slept in
years, poor bastards. And like they wouldn't wake till
Judgment Day. The mess Jesse made killing Hack was
still there. The broken bottle, the trail of milk, a few
miniature bloodstains. The boy decided to clean it up.
No sense in casting even the slightest blame on Jeff.
He went to work with a wet rag and wiped the blood
from the floor. Then he charted the course of milk
marks all the way to the woodstove and halfway up
the wall behind it, wiping as he went. What a mean
milk bottle he swung! He pitched the two halves of

the bottle into the trashcan. Soon he had everything spick-and-span except for the party mess. But that wasn't any of his concern. He had cleaned up his own mess. That was all his old man ever asked of him.

He climbed the stairs to his bedroom and after changing into his pajamas he knelt down to say his prayers. He asked God to watch over Jeff and his old man and Grace and one or two of the kids and his mom in heaven. And then to show he didn't bear any grudges, he asked God not to forget Hack wherever he might be. Because at heart he was a good boy.

PART II
Brothers

ray snowflakes falling like ash from the sky. A dirty morning. The unlit sun hung behind a blockade of cloud. Kitchen jostlings. A table moved. Voices barked. They found the boy in bed with his black tommy gun. He was aiming at a nightmare.

Hack's gone, boy. He say anything to you last night about going off?

I was asleep. With his gun he fired off one last round. That oughter finish the mother, he said to himself.

Truck's still here. He must have left last night or this morning. You didn't see him?

Sure. Shitfaced.

Jesse. Kindly put down that gun and listen. The old man's voice was made of lead. No fun in it. Listen, he repeated. We got to know if Hack said something about where he was going. Anything at all. Gladys is downstairs with Noley. They're a little worried. Afraid Hack might have wandered down by the river or fallen into a cellar hole or something.

Give up. Where is he? In the river? Gone back home? Where?

His old man sighed. That's what we're trying to find out, he said. Where Hack is.

Jesse shouted: Call the police! For he'd love to see one of those Northton squad cars parked in front of the house, its strobe light flashing.

Jeff said: The police got better things to do than look for Hack. That's our job. Find the poor slob . . .

The poor sonofabitch, Jesse corrected him.

Jeff turned with a smile to his father. Sounds like he's been hanging around Hack, he said.

I wish you'd talk to him about using language. He listens to you. . . .

What about the police? the boy demanded.

This is a job for you and me, kid, Jeff said. We'll make a morning of it. Comb the woods . . .

We'll be the police, huh?

That's right. Sergeant Boone reporting for duty, sir. Jeff gave the boy a mock salute.

The old man: Well, I got inspections lined up the wall. If I don't leave now, they'll be hollering for my blood.

He'll turn up, Jeff said to his father. Probably just went out for a little fresh air and couldn't find his way back. You know Hack. When he's plastered, he don't know up from down. Probably went to sleep in a sugarhouse somewhere thinking it was our bedroom.

Jesse waved good-bye to his old man, as was his custom in the morning.

Be waiting for you outside, Chief, Jeff said. And saluted the boy again.

Jesse could see in his brother's manner some-thing of a change from yesterday. It seemed like the old Jeff had come back. He could tell from those nice little salutes. Salutes meant raising hell together. He hopped out of bed and out of his pajamas, holding his shirt in his teeth while eagerly he stepped, first the left leg, then the right, into his trousers. He found he could manage his shoelaces all by himself. Usually he needed help. His problem was he'd skip a hole or pick the wrong hole on the opposite side or the knot would get tied too soon and with such a furor that only by severing the shoelace with a knife could it be undone. No problem now. It was magic what a boy could do with his brother home from Vietnam.

He could think of no better way to spend the day than in search of Hack's body with Jeff. As he left the room, he grabbed his mitt and a baseball. They might want to take time off from their search for a game of pepper. They had done it before, winters ago when they didn't need the excuse of a dead body, only the bright blue-eyed sky luring them to their joy. Jesse remembered it well. Jeff announced: It's time for spring training! And mitts in hand the two brothers had walked through drifts of knee-deep snow right down to the ball field. The little footprints of birds and mice and no doubt rats speckled the field. The sun had turned it into a sea of glittering crystal. Ain't right, Jesse said. What's right or wrong? his brother asked him. It's spring and that means spring training. You're not gonna let a little snow mess with your fun, are you? The boy shook his head. He'd try not to let it mess with his fun. He anchored himself and they started to throw the ball back and forth. But they couldn't get much of a grip on it because their throwing hands were so cold. The ball would fly, fly away and *pock!* fall through the crust of the snow. Jesse observed: It's not catch. . . . He was ready to go home. But then Jeff started diving for the ball and he'd nose-dive into the snow. He'd come up with white scatter-patterns all over his face and coat. Jesse began to do the same thing. Fun, Jeff said. Fun, Jesse repeated. And before long they were throwing the ball away on purpose. To see who was fool enough to make a leap. Jesse was. He began to look like something that had slept the winter out-of-doors. Beneath his feet the

snowy earth crackled like glass. He'd lunge and wait
for his body to crack the surface, falling into the
softer snow which no longer seemed cold at all, but
warm and sandy, like the beach. This is fun! he
shouted. And then he reared back and threw the ball
with such force that it went nowhere, slipped off his
hand and fell between them. And they both dove for
it, they nearly cracked their heads together before
they landed in a huddle, rolling and laughing, two
brothers making a springtime out of the winter. They
wrestled and flung snowballs and pushed each other
down in the snow until the ball field resembled a bat-
tleground where invisible warring bodies had come to
their last rest as snow angels. The brothers came
home drenched in sweat. We'll go there again tomorrow, Jeff promised. But they didn't. Jeff had home-
work.

He took the steps two at a time. His boots
clomped the old wood, which stretched and creaked
as though it were in pain. As for Jesse himself, he was
nowhere near pain. His body seemed to have shed
yesterday's beating with little difficulty. Only an itch-
ing persisted around his mouth and nose, a tickle in
his ribs. The hurt had gone away. Thought the boy:
It's gone to someone else.

He clomped up to the kitchen door. At the table
sat Gladys Newton in her waitress dress. With *Gladys*
written in a swirl of dark yarn above her heart. Hi,
Jesse said.

Jesse. You don't know where Hack is, do you?
the woman asked in a quivery voice.

Dunno, he told her. I went to bed.

To the boy Mrs. Hack was about as ugly as a
woman could be and still be called a woman. Mrs.

Hack had smallpox as a little girl and the craters on her face always made Jesse think of a sponge. Maybe she wasn't a woman at all, maybe she was a sponge. The flabby jowls in which her pockmarks were set looked like they might contract down to practically nothing if a person squeezed them. And her hair looked like it had been used to clean a dirty sink. Jesse couldn't understand what the late Hack had ever seen in her.

She said: He's got a bad heart. His doctor told him to stop drinking, but he never listens. Never listens to anyone. One of these days he's going to drink himself into a heart attack. . . .

You can't blame me, Noley told her. All yesterday I said take it easy on the booze.

Jesse said: He's probally in the river. Bad heart and all.

Noley: Go screw yourself, fellow. Christ Almighty but you give me the creeps sometimes.

The boy didn't think Noley was being fair. He was only repeating what he'd heard from his old man. But dad says Hack's in the river, he declared.

Then Mrs. Hack began to sob softly. Like she was a sponge dripping water. I know he's still alive, she said. I just know it. . . .

A helluva lot you know, thought Jesse. He grabbed his coat and headed for the door. He couldn't stand around all day and watch some dumb woman drench her hanky. He had work to do.

Wait, whimpered the woman.

Bye-bye . . .

Noley yelled after him: Only way he'd get in the river'd be you dumped him there yourself.

And Jesse called back: Liar, liar, pants on fire!

Flecked with snow, his brother was waiting for him beside Hack's truck. The boy hurried over to him. He pounded his ball glove like he meant business. Jeff pointed to the license plate. *Newt*, he said. Funny how he likes that word on his plates. To me a newt is just a little green slimy thing. . . .

To me too, agreed Jesse. Though in truth he couldn't tell a newt from Adam. But he didn't want his brother to think he was a retard.

If I got one of them vanity plates, I'd want a word like *Sport*. Don't you think *Sport*'d be a good word, soldier?

Jesse agreed it would.

And so they set off. Just behind the house they entered a cavern of young birches draped in hoarfrost. They reached a snow-machine track. Suddenly Jeff grasped his brother's wrists. Forceful gentle hands. They could love or kill, depending on what was asked of them. The boy knew what was coming next.

I'm sorry, Jesse. You know I am. Lost control of myself. Dad told me what you did. Only one thing on my mind then. *Get that little fucker* . . . Couldn't help it. I guess it'll be a while before I get used to home again.

Sorry for what? Jesse asked. (He loved every minute of this.)

Don't play dumb. You know what. Beating up on you last night. Geez, didn't even say hello or anything. I just ripped into your room and pounded the living daylights out of you. I bet you thought I was shell-shocked or something. . . .

You ain't shell-shocked, Jeff. . . .

. . . just hope I didn't hurt you too much. You don't look so bad today, but when I saw you last night with all those ripe bruises, shit, I thought, what have I done? Tried to kill my own brother. And I was still too pissed off to say I'm sorry. I'm saying it now.

Didn't mind it a bit.

Don't be a dink, Jesse. . . .

I'm not being a dink. . . .

What're you being then?

. . . a sport . . .

You don't hurt from last night?

Nah. I'm strong.

I don't know as I believe you. . . .

Feel hunnerd percent. Feel like doing a few laps. And he thrust himself through the snow in a kind of slow-motion run, over tangles of trees and blowdown.

His brother caught up with him. You're a tough little bugger, Jeff said. There's guys in my platoon who'd still be bellyaching about the lacing I gave you. Lying in bed and moaning and groaning. You really can take it, kid. . . .

I know, the boy said. He slobbered as would anyone complimented like that. Jesse at the front of his brother's platoon. Jesse goring an enemy belly button with his bayonet. Hero Jesse. Right now he felt like he could swallow a live hand grenade and maybe only belch. For he'd grown a new set of living daylights. Beat the old set out of him and he'd grow new ones again in two shakes. He smacked his ball glove mightily.

His brother saw him. You lose one of your mittens? Jeff asked him.

Nah. I thought we might play some ball.

Play ball? You crazy? It's too damned cold. It's winter out. Wait till spring.

But we done it, Jeff. Had the nicest ball game there ever was . . .

Not in the winter . . .

In the winter, yeah.

Well, I don't remember it. It must have been a long time ago. Do anything when you're just a kid.

It wasn't so long . . .

C'mon now. Where your mittens?

Here. And the boy tucked his ball glove under his belt. In his heart of hearts he knew his brother was right. Practical. Hero Jesse was a soldier, not a kid. And what kind of soldier would rush off into battle with only his ball glove?

By and by their track crossed the tread of another snowmachine. It wound in and out of the trees and disappeared heading west. The tiny food missions of field mice and squirrels were etched into the snow. No other marking disturbed the fresh white coat. Doesn't look like ole Hack's been down here at all, Jeff said.

Probally sleeping it off somewheres.

They crossed the Orem tote road and came upon Fred Orem's sugarhouse, with its wood piled all around the outside. The new snow bundled the little shack. They looked in the window. The syrup tins were stacked up neatly from the year before. In a week or so, it would be sugaring-off time. And Jesse went wild at sugaring-off time. Drinking the unfinished syrup, eating sugar on snow, who but a natural-born idiot would not go wild?

His brother saw him with his eyes aglow and his feet doing a little dance on the white ground. You sure do love the sweet stuff, don't you, Jesse? he said, smiling.

The boy caught that smile. He caught it and kept it. He did dearly love the sweet stuff. He couldn't get enough of it. And he wondered whether they had maple sugar in Vietnam. You go to a lot of sugaring-offs over there? he asked his brother.

In Nam? Hell, no. I don't even believe they got maples over there. Besides it's just too hot. A hundred and ten in the shade. It's like you're trapped inside an oven.

Even in the wintertime?

The sweat drips off you in buckets. You have to take salt pills day and night.

Sounds good to me. . . . Jesse knew he could tolerate a place that was too hot for the sap to run just so long as he could get a good tan and the beaches were nice. He also knew that Grace wouldn't mind. Too much of that sweet stuff would cause all her teeth to fall out anyway. It would make her a tub of lard like the Carnarelli twins. Like him Grace only needed the sun and she'd be happy as a peach.

The track went by a scattering of headstones that comprised the Orem family plot. And as he did whenever he passed this plot, Jesse uttered a silent prayer to the Almighty that in His mercy He see fit to dump Fred and Penny Orem there soon. Jesse guessed that would teach them to mind their own business. For it had been those two who first gave the boy's old man the idea of Concord. They did it at last year's sugaring-off. Nasty thing to happen at a sugaring-off. It happened this way:

Several days after Jeff left for Vietnam, the boy went to the Orems' with his old man. Most of the kids were there already. They were out by the wood-shed drinking sap and making rhymes. Pickles are sour, sugar is sweet, please don't kiss my dirty feet. Syrup and sugar, syrup and sugar, in your nose is a ten-pound booger. Sap, sap, a bottle of sap, the cork falls out and—*it's the sap himself!* They saw Jesse and took off for the sugarhouse, leaving the boy behind like he was a leper. He was ready to chase after them when he saw Penny Orem emerge from the house with her belly all bulged out. He decided to find out whether she had tucked a pillow there or what, it looked so strange. So he put his hand on her stomach and pressed. He expected it would deflate. It didn't. The woman screamed like she'd been stuck with a pitchfork. He's scarred my baby, he's scarred my baby! Raving, she was. What baby? said Jesse. He was trying to show that at least he had all his marbles. You don't got a baby. If you got one, then where is it? But she only screamed and screamed away, Her baby was scarred for life, it'd probably be born with a hump on its back or a twisted leg, she'd have to get some doctor to yank it out now because it wouldn't be fit to live. She was acting like a crazy woman. The boy told her to see the stork if she wanted a baby. Her husband Fred came over and then Jesse knew the whole family was crazy. Shrieked the man: You touch her baby, you little retard? And it was all anyone could do to keep a hold on Fred, who had grabbed a shears. Jesse's old man apologized and said it wouldn't happen again. It won't if you put that little bastard where he belongs, Fred said. Put him down in Concord where he can't go around feeling up pregnant women. Penny agreed through her tears: Rubber room's the only place for a retard like that. . . . The old man only shook his head and led the boy away. But I didn't get any maple creams, Jesse protested.

At the time the boy seldom gave a thought to Concord. He knew it was for sick people and he never expected to see the inside of the place because he never caught colds. But on the trip home from the Orems' he was told it was a different kind of sick. He was told he might have to go to Concord himself. Tears went streaming down his cheeks. There there don't cry boy, his father said softly. If you just behave yourself, you won't need to go there. And Jesse wondered what a person had to do in order to behave himself. He always thought he was behaving himself. From behind his tears he swore at the Orems. He wished Fred's chain saw would spring back and slice off the man's arm and he wished the stork would peck a hole in Penny's stomach. Later he learned that the stork had come along and presented Penny with a baby girl. The baby girl was disfigured neither by a hunchback or a twisted leg. Jesse was a little disappointed.

And now he finished his prayer by asking the Almighty to chuck Reverend in the Orem plot while He was at it. Chuck anyone there who made mention of Concord. The whole town if necessary. Thought the boy: The more, the merrier.

You kill a whole lot of gooks over in Nam, huh, Jeff? Jesse asked his brother.

A few. Not many.

How many?

I don't know, Jesse. Look. You can see the river from here.

The boy looked. Just down the hillock the river appeared, a stout gray serpent sundered in its whole length by the trunks of birch trees. High above he saw the speck of a broadtailed hawk circling after rodenty prey. Do the girls over there really piss in the streets? he asked. Do they, really and truly?

No, they don't. . . .

Hack said they do. . . .

Hack knows how to tell a good story.

Hack said to A-bomb the fucks. Is that all right?

I don't know. I think Charlie's shit is pretty weak now.

We got Charlie on the run?

That's right.

You make him run, Jeff?

Jesse . . .

You see a lot of action, huh, Jeff, didja?

Jesse . . .

I didn't see you on the TV ever at all. . . .

Look, Jesse. I really don't want to talk about it now. All right?

The boy nodded. His brother's face seemed to secrete its war behind a mask hewn from the snow and cold. Plump little snowflakes daubed Jeff's eyebrows, settled on the ridge of his nose. He'll talk later, thought Jesse. A soldier home on leave needs time to recover from the shock of the north country.

There's the old Staley cellar hole, Jeff said. Let's just have a look-see in case Hack's fallen down there.

They stepped through the icestiffened brush and came to a clearing. The gnarled boles of apple trees once marked the ambit of a farmhouse. Staleys had once lived here. The Staley men were bleeders nearly all of whom ended up in the county home. The last Staley died there and the house quickly went to rack and ruin and now only the cellar hole remained, with poplar and maple saplings sprouting out of it.

The brothers regarded the hole from the top of the stone foundation. No Hack lay among the debris. Jeff hopped down, then Jesse, into a pile of ancient planks. The boy picked up the husk of a frozen rabbit by the ears. It was almost weightless. Flying rabbit! he yelled and tossed it at his brother. Quit, Jeff said. He scowled, not wanting to play, half intent on picking through the rubble, like he was searching for something he'd lost, and the other half (so it seemed to the boy) in a kind of waking slumberland. He's still getting used to home, thought Jesse. He chased a mouse to a chink in the wall, which he sealed off with a rock. He toppled a tinsel baby buggy. Off in a corner a beam lay athwart an old bedstead like a vengeful weapon against sleep. The boy wondered if some unwitting Staley hadn't once been crushed to death by that beam. He tried jumping on a section of the rusted spring, but it no longer had any bounce. He kicked it. Then he noticed what looked like a set of giant upturned teeth. What's that? he asked. Pointing. Wary.

An old harrow, his brother told him.

A harrow . . .

They once used it to break up the ground and smooth it off.

Silly. What for?

Farmers. They use a harrow when they're dragging a field. Staleys were farmers and this was once their farmland. Pretty choice farmland, too. Hard to believe with all these trees.

Can't farm trees, Jesse declared.

Well, it wasn't always like this. They had it cleared almost down to the river. But they couldn't manage it, what with so many bleeders in the family and all.

The boy giggled uneasily. No wonder the Staleys bled so much. With these sharp teeth always bared and lying in wait for them. He was glad he was born a Boone, not a Staley.

They returned to the track. Ain't found him yet, Jesse said.

I bet Hack's down at the Cartier this very moment, Jeff told him. I bet he's having a pretty good laugh on us right now.

Getting wiped out!

The track ended and a more narrow path proceeded from it, zigzagging along the bluffs. Now the entire scope of the river was visible, from the snowy banks rising on the opposite side all the way down to the Hollow, where the Canucks lived, lean wisps of smoke straggling up from their shacks. Craning his neck Jesse tried to locate the spot where he and Margaret had their fun.

They descended. The path corkscrewed around boulders. Now and then it was still frozen over. Bad footing. Jesse had never been able to walk on ice without falling down. This time was no exception. Soon he went head-over-ass like a candlepin and landed in the prickles of a berry bush. Motherfucker, he hissed at the bush. After that he held on to his brother's arm. Jeff slowed his pace to accommodate the boy. And Jesse, because he liked holding on to his brother, slowed his own pace to make the adventure last longer.

As they walked Jeff's mouth moved slowly, like the mouth of a very old man. He said: You know when you asked me about the war, Jesse? I didn't mean to give you a hard time. It's just real hard for me to talk about that stuff. It's hard to find the right words that'll give you a true picture of it. Know what I mean?

Calflike the boy stared over at his brother. He didn't seem to understand. He tried to scratch his head through his mittens. But I got words, he said.

Remember a couple of winters ago when Bob Siddall got frostbit so bad? He blew his nose and it came off in his hand? Well, let's say you're Bob and you're looking down at that nose in your hand. Hell, what can you say? *Lookit here I just lost my nose?*

Replied the boy: You told me it was steaming

hot. How can a person be frostbit and his nose fall off if it's steaming hot?

No, Jesse. You don't get it.

I get it. You got wounded in action and had to pick up a new nose. The boy looked at what he took to be his brother's new nose and it seemed to him a good fit.

Same old nose, Jeff smiled. And I wasn't wounded at all. Less you call stepping on a punji stick wounded.

A punji stick . . .

Yeah. They're made of bamboo and sharpened at one end. Charlie bakes this shit, real shit, into them and covers them with dirt and leaves. Step on one and you get a bad infection. It's like stepping on a rusty nail.

That's all the wounded you got? No bullet holes or nothing?

Hell, I didn't see a whole lot of action. I was in a recon platoon. Sneak and retreat stuff. I wrote you that. We made a few raids on villages about the size of Hollinsford. Small.

Didn't you even see any dead people?

Jesse, you oughter get something straight. It's not the TV. It's ugly. People with their heads blown off, their heads popped like melons. Makes you really think. You know what I mean? You see some dead guy and there's, well, nothing there. You sort of ask yourself, Is that all? I mean, you're dead and that's it. Just brains and gore, that's all we got.

Brains and gore, the boy repeated in a casual voice, like he had known all along that was all a person had.

By now they had reached the bottom. Stepping carefully they came up to the river. Fanged waterfalls of ice fell without motion over the low shore face. But the river ice seemed to be crumbling. And it was warmer down here. The snow had abated, though if the sun existed it was buried in a sky the color of dead clay.

Whoooie! Jeff exclaimed. It's harder climbing down than climbing up. Could use me a couple of beers right now.

Me, I could use a couple of milks.

Jeff laughed. Not much danger of you ending up like Hack, that's for sure.

You mean dead. . . .

Dead drunk, I mean. Stick to your milk. Better for you.

Then why do you stick to beer?

I'm dumb. Headed for an early grave, haha . . .

Me, too . . .

You're just saying that because I did.

Right.

They walked downstream to a jungle of alders whose grasping roots hugged what the river discarded, brush, pieces of siding, broken window frames, raggedy clothes, and certain tree parts that were shaped like viscera. The brothers sat down to rest on a thick alder root flexed from its trunk like a biceps muscle. And Jesse began to toy with what looked to him like a bikini top, trying to tear it loose from where it was raveled around the root.

Main reason I didn't see more action (Jeff went on) was this turkey of a CO I had named Shanahan. Ralph Shanahan, from Dayton, Ohio. Weird as the day is long. Guy had this cobra tattoo on his arm and I swear, he talked to the thing, soft cooing noises like it was a baby.

This Shanahan from around here? the boy asked. His eyes little slits of suspicion.

I told you. He's from Ohio. That's west of here a little. And he nearly split a gut when he heard I was from New Hampshire. Never met anyone from New Hampshire before. He picked on me because he thought I was a hick. Boone, he said, you should be real comfortable out here in the boonies. . . .

Wouldn't want him on my team. . . .

And this Shanahan, he thought he was real tough. He told us how to crack the rib cage and pull the heart out of a man. But deep down he was pansy-assed. He was afraid of fighting. He always got us to cover for some other platoon. That's what recon means. Trailing some other guy's shadow. They'd dust off some hooches or whatever and we'd dash in and clean up the mess. Sometimes we'd even steal the other guy's body count. You know what a body count is?

Sure. Dead gooks. This Shanahan really steal dead gooks?

Well, not quite like that. Think of football. Let's say every time you make a touchdown, the ref gives it to the other team. You wouldn't call that fair, would you?

Said Jesse: I'd nail that ref with an M-60. As at last he had the bikini thing loose and in his pocket.

I wouldn't go that far. But this guy was a real jolterhead. Can't get much lower than Ralph Shanahan . . .

Torpedo the mother . . .

. . . treated me like I was dirt. Had me washing dishes and building latrines all the time. He sent me off on these dumb corpse patrols, counting bodies morning, noon, and night. Like I wasn't smart enough for anything else . . . .

Torpedo his balls off . . .

. . . and when there wasn't no dead bodies around, he'd break his back to find them. Dig them up out of the ground. Once we came to this village that'd been evacuated. They must have smelled us coming. Nothing around except a few water buffalo. Shanahan said shoot them and we did. Then he had us boobytrap them with C-4 charges so if Charlie came back to get the meat, he'd be blown to Kingdom Come. Well, we're in this village and there's not a single body in sight, dead or alive, except the buffaloes we just shot. Shanahan is mad as hops. He starts ordering me to dig up these graves. . . .

Just like back home! Jesse exclaimed. Remember when you dug up old man Scoggins, Jeff? He asked were there many old graves in Vietnam.

Jeff said: You don't go over there to screw around with dead bodies. You go to defend your country.

You screwed dead bodies? Dead *girls'* bodies?

Jesse . . .

Was it on the TV? Didn't see it.

Kindly keep quiet. You were the one that wanted to hear all this. . . .

OK, the boy said. I'll keep my trap shut. But that didn't mean he would keep his eyes closed as well. He began to search the woods for some sign of those cunning gooks. It wasn't like them to let a whole village fall into our hands without a fight.

You have just got to learn to listen, Jeff said. I was telling you about these graves. Now, Charlie buries his dead above the ground. In sorta these mounds. But in this one little village they had a graveyard American-style, with these new-looking tombstones. Turkey Shanahan took one look at this graveyard and he walked over to me and said, Boone, see what's in them graves. He thought maybe a secret store of weapons was buried there. . . .

The boy knew that the gooks wouldn't waste good weapons by throwing them in some dirty old grave. How dumb can you get? He knew trouble lurked nearby.

. . . well, this ground hasn't been touched in years. I'm no grave robber, I told him. You stupid grunt, he said—that's what your ordinary soldier is called, a grunt. You stupid grunt, fuck on over there and dig up those graves or you'll be digging latrines for the next month. So I dig down two feet and come to this coffin. Shanahan ordered me to break it open and I did, and nothing was there, just a little dust. I broke open three or four more coffins which had old bones, skeletons, in them. And Geeze if those skeletons didn't join our body count. That's how our platoon got such a high body count. Makes you want to puke up Jonah.

The storm of battle rather than Jonah was welling up inside the boy. He knew the empty village and plastic skeletons were only a slanteyed trick. To put the platoon off its guard. He was no dummy. But all Shanahan did was rearrange his privates and yawn. A lack of dead bodies made him sleepy. A few grunts were playing poker. And Jeff was still at work digging up graves, a sitting duck for any sniper.

Hero Jesse stood sentry over the entire group of them, black tommy gun in hand, alone of all that platoon open-eyed and alert. Silently he glared up the rocky slope and the thicket beyond it, hoping to catch a glimmer of a rifle, some sign of Charlie in the wilderness. Then he heard sniper fire. Jeff, he yelled, take cover! Snipers!

Don't be silly, Jesse. That's only the ice breaking upstream. Water's deeper there. You're not afraid of ice, are you?

Gunfire hit a booby-trapped buffalo and the animal exploded and buffalo eyes and ears and pieces of hide and intestines rained down on the terrified grunts. Another sharp *crack!* and a bright red spray of blood spurted out from Shanahan's head and the big man crumpled to the ground with his hand still in his jockstrap. The boy watched with a certain indifference as a large shell landed *bammm!* near Shanahan's body and its force lifted up Jeff's nasty CO and sent him flying through the air like a little feathery whirligig. That your ice? the boy hollered over to his brother. And Jeff gave him a quick respectful smile, like, Geez, Hero Jesse really knew war from Shinola, and dropped down to the ground. He crawled into a convenient grave to sit this one out. Let his brother do the fighting.

And then the Hero told the enemy that they had had their fun.

Jesse with a tommy gun bigger than the President's braced pleasantly against his body, crouched forward a-soldiering. Keen bird-of-prey eyes trained on a clump of trees high above the river. In which he could at last see his target, a legion of yellow skins perched on the tree branches like a roost of canaries. Thought Jesse: It may be their village, but it's my war. And with that he opened up fire on them. *Rat-a-tat-tat, rat-a-tat-tat, rat-a-tat-tat!* His brother told him to shut up, he was making a racket. His brother told him it was only the ice cracking. *Rat-a-tat-tat, rat-a-tat-tat!* His faithful gun sang like it'd been waiting to sing for days. Shit Jesse, you stop that, his brother said. But the boy couldn't stop now. He was having too much fun. Out of the trees the little gooks began to fall, a trickle at first, then a steady stream of them. *Rat-a-tat-tat!* Shot by a demon marksman, they cleared the boulders and they pirouetted like airborne dancers into the river, shouting and screeching, swept up by strong waters. *Jesse!* A brother's angry hand clamped to his shoulder, tugging at him. Now the last of the gooks were somersaulting into the river, their faces all bloodsmirched and their arms and legs awry. Who would have thought that so many of them could die from the fire of only one soldier?

Jeff said: Jesse, that's disgusting. Jerking off like that. You oughter be ashamed of yourself. Right here in broad daylight. I'm taking you home right now.

But it isn't broad daylight. It's clouds and gray sky.

Shit, you know what I mean.

I didn't do nothing, the boy protested.

Didn't do nothing? You just jerked off sitting right here beside me. And you even look proud of it. Hell, I don't know what's wrong with you. . . .

And unseen by either of them, jiggled loose from Jesse's belt, was his ball glove, which landed on the thin ice at the edge of the river.

They walked through the scrub beside the river, Jeff leading, Jesse lingering a few steps behind. Chickadees scattered for them and fluttered back once they'd passed, whistling *sizzle-ee, sizzle-ee.* Soon they were thrashing through a blackberry thicket and then a snowed-in stretch of pastureland. Cold feet. And soon after that they reached the bridle path, which hadn't seen a horse in twenty years, hardly much else, only Jesse's fun with Margaret.

Jeff gestured brusquely to his brother to speed it up. He pointed to the path. Following it they'd get home in a fraction of the time they'd take heading back up the rise and through the woods. And Jesse was glad to take that path. It bore rich memories.

Along the way the boy couldn't resist crunching patches of exposed witch grass with his boots. The little spikes of frost made a sound like soft shattered crystal. He liked that sound. He liked it so much that Jeff was way ahead of him. Then Jeff turned and saw him crunching away like he didn't have a care in the world. He grabbed the boy by his fur collar and said, I've just about had as much from you as I can take. Next time I speak to you it's gonna be with my hand. You hear? I got better things to do than sit back and smile at your dumb little games. Now get down this path right away. Stop shackling about. Remember last night?

Christmas but Jeff had a hair across his ass! Jesse knew his brother hadn't appreciated his display back there among the alders. But Jeff must have seen worse in Vietnam. Our boys with their heads blown open, nothing there except gore. Girls pissing in the streets. Something about Vietnam made the boy's brother finicky. Mean-spirited. And Jesse knew what it was: not enough action. You'll do more killing next time, he comforted Jeff.

Shut up, Jesse.

Poor Jeff! Other soldiers from other families had hogged it all. They appeared on the TV. They napalmed villages maybe even bigger than Concord. And Jeff had to sit it out on the sidelines. High of hope he'd gone away to war and instead of action he ended up robbing graves. A person could rob graves at home. With better results, too.

Walking beside his brother now, the boy recalled Jeff's New Hampshire grave-robbing adventure. He wished he'd taken part in it, but hearing it firsthand from Jeff was almost as good. The adventure started with Mr. Vandecar, the bastard. He caught Jeff and

Noley stealing a few nubbins of corn and took them to court. They had to shell out fifty dollars apiece in fines and court fees. Jesse had never seen his brother so wicked angry as when he came back from court that day. At dinner he swore he'd get Mr. Vandecar and get him but good. The old man only shook his head as was his custom and said he hadn't raised his son to be a thief. Jeff said it was only corn. And afterwards he went off and met Noley and together they drove away in Hack's pickup. They headed up Sugarhill Road to the old Scoggins plot. The plot was so out of the way that the day Jasper Scoggins was buried, the hearse got lost looking for it. So the boys didn't worry about getting caught. With their shovels they went to work on the five-month-old grave. They figured that old man Scoggins at five months would be quite ripe. Neither too firm nor too moldy. And they were dead right. The Scoggins family hadn't been able to afford more than a wooden box. By now it was gone. Jeff and Noley found themselves face-to-face with something green and cheesy. Head smooth as a ball. Reptile claws for hands. Plates of fungus such as grow on decayed logs. A bow tie. Right away they knew Jasper Scoggins was perfect. They knew he'd make a terrific splash. As they began to roll him up with their shovels, green lumps of skin dropped off. Take it easy, Jeff said. We have to save some for Mr. Vandecar. They put the body in a gunnysack. And the stink from that sack nearly made them both puke. Jasper's not had a bath in five months, Jeff said. By the time they reached the Vandecar estate, it was pitch-dark outside. Gently they eased the body from its sack and into the swimming pool. Noley shone his flashlight on it. Jasper had sunk to the bottom and was sort of hovering there like some huge slow-mov-

ing fish. Jeff declared: Hope he don't swim away. And
he didn't swim away. He was still there the next
morning when Mr. Vandecar went in for a dip. And
Jeff heard that when the man found the whopping
load of carrion that had been Jasper Scoggins clogging
his filter, he nearly drowned. They needed smelling
salts to revive him. And he didn't use his swimming
pool ever again because it made him think of dead
bodies. For which he blamed the Canucks. They were
to blame for most crimes around town. The county
police questioned every Frenchman in the Hollow but
without much luck except for finding Pierre the Pisser
with five gallons of rotgut home brew. That's great!
Jesse would say then settle back and await the punch
line. Yeah, Jeff would reply, and nearly as funny was
when Noley got home the night of our prank. Hack
took one whiff of his pickup and said, Whoooee! You
been drinking, boy?

This exploit of Jeff's was the boy's favorite bed-
time story. Sometimes Jeff would be asked to tell the
story three or four times the same night. Jesse never
seemed to get tired of it as he got tired of the fairy
tales his old man told him. Those fairy tales weren't
about his brother.

Tell me about digging up Jasper Scoggins, will
you, Jeff? the boy asked.

I've told you that stupid story a thousand times if
I told it once.

I know. But I want to hear it again. Kindly, Jeff.

You're not hearing no story. Every time I open
my mouth, you go off and do something crazy. . . .

What something crazy do you mean?

Like what you did back there, for instance. Jerking off . . .

. . . that was gooks . . .

Shitfire, said Jeff.

The boy knew that not enough action made a person sour as swill. He'd be nasty himself if what had happened to Jeff had happened to him. War shouldn't make a person snotnosed. Jesse's war wouldn't. Jesse's war would have action for all. Gooks aplenty for the young and old, rich and poor alike. No complaints. His old man had often sat him down and lectured him about fair. The good Lord dished out equal portions to everyone, boy. Worms, dad? Did He give worms equal portions? The old man: Worms got their place, you got yours, I got mine. It isn't right to take what isn't yours because when you do that, you're stealing from God Himself. God was Jesse's friend and so he stopped taking cookies that weren't his. Certain other folks were less nice. They hogged all the cookies. All the gooks, too.

C'mon, Jesse. Cut bait. We don't got all day. Stop inspecting every little turd or plant you see.

The boy decided his brother needed cheering up. He said: Let's hit the Miracle Mile, Jeff! Tear the town up, huh . . .

Only thing I'm gonna hit is you if you don't stop dawdling.

Kindly don't hit me. I only want to cheer you up.

You can cheer me up by keeping your mouth shut and by not walking like you got a truckload of shit in your pants.

You used to like me talking. Before you went away . . .

I ain't changed a fig. You're the one who's changed. . . .

Gotten big as a horse, huh?

Have it your way, buster. . . .

. . . but I want to have it your way . . .

Then just gimme a little peace, all right?

Hack said only if we A-bomb the fucks . . .

Jee-sus!!!

At which point the boy noticed his ball glove was missing and he lurched back along the path searching for it.

What the hell is wrong now? his brother shouted to him.

I lost my . . . And he stopped in mid-sentence. Did he really care about that moth-eaten hunk of leather? His brother had told him the ball glove was silly. And so it was. He grinned.

Lost what?

Lost my wind. But I found it again.

In the distance the buzzer sounded the afternoon shift at the broom-handle factory, a hoarse urgent call. All at once Jeff went white and ducked down. Geez, he said, though not to Jesse, sounds like our warning signal. . . . He got up again but the boy was still bent down, his hands tucked behind his head, prepared for the worst.

The brothers came into Hollinsford attended by the stonemason's shriveled yellow cur and went up one street and down the other (there were only two streets), arriving in the center of town just after the broom-handle factory had let out.

Frog alert, Jesse whispered to his brother.

And then in an instant they were all gone, those dark half-shaven faces, sucked up into the Cartier Club. The town looked like it was up for sale. Dead or not yet born. To the boy the town had soft unmoving legs on Saturday afternoons. It was then that most people went to Northton for their shopping. Not Jesse. Saturday afternoon was when his old man let him wander the streets. If the streets were empty.

Past the raucous laughter of the Cartier they marched and into the Heritage Spa & Gift Shoppe. The high-school hangout. Stay here, buster, Jeff told his brother. I'm going back for a few beers, and you better be here when I return. Then he went over to Iris Carnarelli, the owner's wife, who was settled at the counter with the *Union-Leader*. Gladys here? he asked her.

She went to Bethel with Noley, the woman said. Drove there around noon. Her husband run off from her.

He's missing. . . .

Probably off with some hussy somewhere. I wouldn't put it past that man.

Hack ain't been found, then?

Well, I don't know. The police called up and Gladys was out of here like a shot. I don't think they found him, though.

He'll turn up. Anyway, give Jesse here a glass of milk and some kind of sandwich, Jeff said. He left a dollar on the counter. Before he headed out he looked hard at the boy. Mind what I told you about staying put, he said.

Promise, Jesse answered.

Iris Carnarelli slapping together some kind of sandwich. Beefy hands among bread slices and jars of what smelled like paste. Jesse stared, but not at the sandwich ingredients. The Carnarelli woman fascinated him. Maybe if she didn't have a mustache, she'd be only another woman. But she did have that mustache and it squiggled there above her lip like a little caterpillar. Jesse often wondered did she have a cock as well. Otis Dimick said no (though he did say she cut her corns with a fish knife). But Jesse wasn't so sure. He still had so much to learn about females. Staring helped him to learn. He stared at the flesh

around Iris Carnarelli's thighs for some sign of a
bulge. A bulge would not have surprised him.

Thought the boy: Maybe her husband Sal has
one of those pussies.

She passed him his milk and sandwich. And
what are you looking at? she said.

You wear a jockstrap? he asked her.

She gave him one evil scowl but said nothing. He
guessed the answer to his question was yes. He didn't
pursue it for he didn't want to embarrass the woman
any further. No one could say he wasn't sensitive to
other people's feelings.

Jesse found a seat next to one occupied, blimp-
like, by one of the Carnarelli twins. Right away the
girl made a shrill noise that was meant to be a giggle.
It never failed. Whenever they saw him, the twins
giggled. Something about him struck them as funny.
Jesse figured they were only trying to cover up their
true feelings. He figured they had a king-size crush on
him. They were bowled over by his TV face and they
were eager to get their teenage paws on his sleek
body. It was not unlikely. Others had succumbed to
his charms.

He sat facing the pinball machines. From where
he was sitting he could get a good view of the famous
Heritage toilet stalls. Whoever built the place had not
seen fit to conceal these stalls, which lay right behind
the pinball machines. A person could see feet standing in there, and feet dangling, and sometimes even
more. From time to time bad smells would float
through to the restaurant side.

Sometimes Jesse would roll a penny under one of
these machines to get a better look. He wasn't the
only one. No less a person than Raymond Perkins
was known around town as a real whizbang at the job.

He was so skillful that he'd never been caught. Beaver shooting, he called it. And the boy had tried to imagine a beaver squatting in a stall in the Heritage Spa, but he couldn't. Beavers used his friend the great out-of-doors. When he conveyed this fact to Raymond, he was told that he was dumber than a stump. But Raymond himself once admitted to Jeff that he'd never really seen a decent beaver at the Heritage. Jesse had never seen any sort of beaver there. Once his penny rolled right into the stall and he found himself gazing up at the surprised face of Miss Searton, the schoolteacher. The old woman let out a shriek and tried to kick him. To the boy she was neither a beaver nor anything else.

Bulky legs now protruded. Tree trunks. Jesse figured they belonged to the other twin. There was no mistaking the Carnarelli family flab. It hogged stalls, tables, sidewalks, wherever it chanced to be. Noley once said that the only place for the Carnarellis was a warm shitpile. Wallowing. Eyetalians love shitpiles even more than Canucks, Noley said.

The toilet flushed and out came Sondra (Rose?) to join her sister, giggling as was her custom when she saw Jesse. He gave them both pleasant nods, each in her turn. Good manners prevented him from letting on that he thought them a pair of Berkshire hogs. The twins noticed he was nodding and smiling at them and they returned to their sodas. But soon they were peeping over at him again, little curious darkeyed glances. They love me, Jesse thought. He could hardly blame them. Puffing up his chest he said: I'm going to Vietnam to fight. . . .

One of the twins, guffawing, sent a spray of strawberry soda all the way across the table.

. . . and defend our country, the boy added.

Waves of laughter. Their bodies wobbled like jello. Rose (Sondra?) mentioned something about getting only as far as the funny farm and then blew him a kiss, which was all the invitation he needed. Kisses had but one purpose in Jesse's scheme of things. You girls screw? he whispered.

Apparently they didn't hear him. They were too busy sucking at their sodas. Now Jesse looked at them with genuine interest. Rumor had it that they did screw though not in the normal way. Noley said they did it with coke bottles. No doubt they hadn't come across Mr. Right yet. It'd be hard to find a Mr. Right, Jesse reckoned, when you're a Carnarelli tub of lard. For a Carnarelli the only Mr. Right was a coke bottle. Until now.

Their tits were shaped like grocery bags, but it didn't take much to turn the boy's thoughts to love. He knew he could use the practice. It'd be for Grace's sake as much as for his own. Right now he was a tenderfoot except for Margaret. He could barely tell poontang from toothpaste. His girl mightn't appreciate that. She might tell him to get lost. Grace: You can't hit the broad side of a barn with that thing. What Jesse needed now more than anything else was a little target practice. And the twins would be his barn.

Give you a quarter if you let me see your whatsy, the boy said, turning from one twin to the other. He thought that the best approach. Go one step at a time, shine up to them first.

What's a whatsy?

You know. What you peepee with . . .

They didn't seem to like this idea. He could tell because they stopped giggling. A nervous silence ensued. They retreated into a huddle. Then one of them said to him, A quarter isn't enough.

Don't got nothing more.

Well, for a quarter all you get to see is the bottom of my shoe. She raised her shoe for him to gaze at.

No fair, he protested. I can see that for free.

Know something he can see for a quarter? the girl asked her sister.

You could show him your stamp collection. . . .

I could do that. I bet he'd really like to see my stamp collection.

I would not, Jesse said.

One of the girls leaned forward and in a hushed voice she said: I'll let you see my bra. And as the boy's eyes brightened she added: But for a quarter you only get to see the straps.

Jesse was bewildered by all this female talk. He didn't quite know how to take it. Finally he said: I'll show you *mine.*

Who wants to see that old thing?

It's not old. It's newer than yours.

Then one of them—probably Rose, for she was the bolder of the two—looked him straight in the eye and declared, Now if you had fifty cents, I guess I'd show you *anything* you wanted.

Only Jesse would not have known the girl was teasing. He nearly broke out in a sweat right then and there. He thought about all those acres of flesh that he'd be able to roam. Eagerly he replied: I'll go and get it from my brother.

Oh no! It's now or never. . . .

He was not one to mince words or bargain over terms. He took the girl at face value. He stood up and went over to her table. His hands splayed across a full palette of food stains. The twins, giggleless again, cringed. Hurtling toward them was a winning smile. Kindly give me some pussy, Jesse blurted out loudly.

Iris Carnarelli rushed over. Fuzzy lips all atwitter. You get away from my daughters, she squealed. You just get away from them. Talking like that to young girls. You sick little boy! You should be ashamed of yourself.

I didn't do nothing. . . .

Lord only knows what would have happened next!

I only asked . . .

The twins exclaimed: Dummy was gonna hit us.

You just scram out of here, the woman said. Go on. Out you go. I wouldn't have let you in except you were with your brother.

But I promised . . .

She shooed him out the door. A woman who didn't give a plugged nickel about promises. The hairy old bitch. And don't you ever come in here again! she shouted after him, slamming the door so hard the eagle emblem nearly fell off. The boy gave her the finger but it did no good.

Jesse proceeded down to the Cartier Club. He was a bit upset. For he was not a person to go back on a promise, especially a promise to his brother. He wanted Jeff to respect him and what respect is due someone who says he'll stay put and then doesn't? Might as well bury your head in the ground, boy, like an owl or whatever.

The Cartier was off limits to him. His old man thought it unwise for him to mingle with the broom-handle workers and brute loggers who bided there. But now he had to mingle. Otherwise his poor brother would be racked with worry. If he wasn't sitting back in the Spa, Jeff would think he'd been run over or kidnapped or maybe even murdered.

He pushed open the big iron door and passed

through a vestibule pooled with melted snow and there he was, not much of a Hero now, beset by cigarette smoke and loud Canuck yakety-yak. He nearly backed out again. He couldn't even see Jeff in the midst of all this hubbub. So he simply stood there by the door, stone-still, the strange place riding roughshod over him. At last someone called his name and pointed out his brother sitting off by himself in a corner. Slowly the boy walked over to him. He took care not to touch a Canuck. The kids said a person could get warts from Canucks.

When Jeff noticed him, he looked the other way. The boy sat down and eased close to his brother. Hi, he said.

Don't you know you're not allowed in here?

I know. But they kicked me out of the Spa.

Kicked you out? Geez, what'd you do now?

Nothing. Only I was a sick little boy. . . .

You threw up in there? Shit.

Nah. Wouldn't do a thing like that. I only tried to be friends with those fat twins.

Jeff looked around. He did not seem proud to be seen with the boy. He took a quick draft from his mug and closed his eyes. You didn't try to . . . assault them, did you, Jesse? he asked.

Assault. What's that mean, Jeff?

Means screw, you dink. Screw. You get it now?

Didn't get that far. They wanted to show me their stamp collection. But I didn't want no stamp collection. I wanted pussy.

In one gulp Jeff finished his beer. C'mon, he said. We're getting the hell out of here.

Where we going now? How about to Northton, huh?

Jesse followed his brother to the door. He hap-

pened to touch a Canuck and at once warts sprouted
in his mind and he knew he'd better wash soon, else
they'd spread to his arms and legs. He didn't want
that. If he was seen with warts, he mightn't be
shipped out to Vietnam. The army wouldn't want him
to spread those warts to our boys over there. Straightaway he started washing with the sidewalk slush.

Jeff hurried into the Spa. A few minutes later,
having tallied the damage the boy had done, he came
back out looking mad as a hornet. They had only
gone a few steps when he turned and screamed, Jesse
marked it well because it was so unlike his brother to
scream, except at a ball game. And this is what he
screamed: Goddamn you, Jesse! You know where you
belong? You belong in the loony bin! That's right,
Concord! And if I had my way, that's where you'd be
this very moment—locked up. . . .

Two brothers heading back home, past Perley
Dimick the stonemason's yard and past the hardware
store and the pizza palace and Homer's Barber Shop,
now shut for good. Up the steep hill they went,
through cindery slush and runoff. Jesse trailed a little
distance behind his brother. He couldn't rid himself
of what Jeff said about Concord. He moved in a
weight of distress. He wanted to go back into the
woods and lie there and pretend to be dead until Jeff
was sorry.

Jesse felt a little better when he saw the police car
parked in front of the house. Not since Officer Granville and the outhouse had the law bothered to call on
the Boone family. It was about time they decided to
pay another visit.

He didn't want to miss a detail, a single grue-
some detail. He dashed through the door and slung

off his coat. Hair slicked back, shirt tucked in, he followed the voices into the living room. Jeff and his father sat in chairs flanking the couch, which the officer occupied all by himself. Sitting, as he should, in the seat of honor. A bonechocked Marine's face, ropy with muscle. The officer's eyes looked up at him from a cup of coffee. Jesse regarded not those eyes but the officer's gun. He wished the man would pass it around for them to admire. That a Colt .45? he inquired.

Jesse, this is Deputy Gagnon. He's a county officer. He's here about Hack.

How do you do, Jesse?

Fine. You catch the killer yet?

His old man turned to the deputy. The boy spends too much time in front of the TV, he said. He thinks everything's murder and violence.

Well, said Deputy Gagnon, I'd still like to ask him and his brother a few questions. For the records, you know. It's necessary to talk to the whole family in cases like this one. You never know who might turn up some useful piece of information.

Of course. Ask them anything you want. The old man looked reluctantly at Jesse. He winced, as though he expected the boy would incriminate them all.

Deputy Gagnon brought out his notebook. He fixed first Jeff, then Jesse, with his sharp blue eyes. The boy felt a tremor of delight pass through his body. It tapped at the nook in his brain where the Hero slept. The deputy said: First of all, I'd like to find out what you know about a logger named Andy Holderness. . . .

He jacks deer, Jesse volunteered. Got but one eye. Buckshot in the other. Jacks deer all the same.

The old man shook his head wearily.

That's Andy's brother Phillip, Jeff told the dep-

uty. Though there's not much to choose from between them. They're two of the worst punks in the
county. I went to school with Andy. He used to
threaten the teachers with his penknife. Sold home
brew to little kids. He was four times in seventh
grade. Been in and out of trouble ever since I've
known him.

He wasn't around here last night, was he?

Andy? Hell, no. Wouldn't let a guy like that into
the house.

Did Mr. Newton and him get along?

Nobody gets along with Andy Holderness. Why?

Well, we picked up this Holderness fellow with
Hack Newton's wallet this morning. You don't have
any idea how he could have come by it, do you?

Jesse chimed in: Murdered Hack and took his
wallet! He was proud that he had put two and two
together like that. He glanced around, expecting ap-
proval, heads nodding as if to say, Should have been a
cop, that boy. But those heads nodded not at all. Deputy Gagnon told him not to jump to conclusions.

Where'd he find the wallet? Jeff said.

He says he found it on the back road to Northton. You think Mr. Newton could have dropped it on
the road last night? Dropped it maybe on the way to
visit a friend?

Yeah, maybe. But it was cold. Hack would have
taken his truck.

Even if he was in no condition, let's say, to drive?

Any road and Hack'd take his truck. He takes it
everywhere. He'd take it into bed with him if it'd fit
through the door.

No place, no friend's house, where you think he
might be, you know, sleeping it off?

Thought Jesse: Too many corpses in the man's
routine. He's gotten tired of it all. That's why he can't
find a Hack in a haystack. The boy decided to enliven
things a bit.

Just what was his condition like when you last
saw him? Deputy Gagnon said to Jeff. How much
drink had he taken?

Jesse at the TV, turning it on and switching the
knob to—

Jeff said: He was really loaded. It was only beer,
but he must have had, wait, let's see, a couple down in
Portsmouth . . .

—*Saturday afternoon wrassling!*

. . . two or three in Dover, Rochester, then we
took a detour to Salmon Falls to see his old army
buddy Bill Flint, a couple there . . .

Jesse couldn't care less about all that beer. He
bent forward in his chair to watch the grimacing roly-
poly wrasslers. His eyes followed each dropkick, flip,
and headbutt. He clapped his hands in delight when
he saw that one of them had the other in what looked
like a death-dealing figure-four leglock. The boy got
up and stood next to the TV in order to study death at
first hand.

. . . probably a six-pack here . . .

And to his chagrin he only got to see the two
men separate and return to their respective corners.

. . . let's see, that makes twenty, twenty-two cans
of beer, I guess.

—*Chief Ivan Strongbow and his archenemy the execu-
tioner!*

That's a lot of beer, the deputy whistled.

Seconds after the sound of the bell Strongbow
was in the center of the ring grappling with the Execu-

tioner's mask. *It could be, I believe, fans,* the announcer yelled. *I think this evil man is finally gonna get unmasked.* The men tilted and fell.

Get it, rip off that mask, hollered Jesse, shaking his fist at the TV.

Jesse, please, the old man said. We got a police officer here and he's trying to conduct an investigation.

I already solved it, the boy stated.

Deputy Gagnon merely laughed at him. He went on laughing as Chief Strongbow struggled in vain to remove the mask. Well, he said, I really don't have any more questions. . . .

Don't you got any for me? the boy inquired.

The deputy patted him on the back. You've done real well with the questions I've given you, he said.

That's cause I'm a soldier, Jesse replied proudly.

Jesse! Jeff's voice had a fist in it.

The old man got the deputy's coat. What do we do now? he asked the man.

Play a waiting game. When Holderness sobers up, he may be able to say some more about how he came in possession of that wallet. Put the polygraph on him. Guy was so drunk, he plowed his jeep into the First Congregationalist Church in Bethel. And that takes some doing, I'm here to tell you. The building lies about a hundred feet off the road.

Jesse was at the TV again. You wanna see some war? he asked the man.

No, Jesse. I'm afraid I have to be on my way now.

The boy didn't want to see Deputy Gagnon go. He still wanted to talk corpse with the man. Of which he had some experience himself. He'd like to share some of his thoughts and hear stories from a man whose business was corpses. It was a business he admired. He wished his old man had gone into it instead of cars. He said: Please stay, mister. Pretty please with sugar on it . . .

That's the nicest invitation I've heard all day, Jesse. But I really got to be on my way now. I got other cases I need to attend. There's some guy that's been poisoning dogs over in Lyman. You don't want to see a guy like that running around loose, do you?

Hand grenade's better than poison, the boy said, hoping to lure the deputy into a conversation.

What?

For getting rid of dogs. Or one of them C-4 charges. That's good, too. . . .

Jeff was at the TV and he turned off the wrasslers so violently that the knob came loose in his hand. He threw up his arms in disgust. Like that was his brother's fault, too.

Well good luck anyway, the old man said hurriedly, as though he wanted to spare the deputy any further acquaintance with his family. I hope you get your man. *Both* your men. That dog killer, too.

Oh he's probably just some old hunter who doesn't like dogs savaging his deer. That's all.

Now's the time for those dogs, all right.

Sure is, the deputy said. And don't worry too much about Mr. Newton. If he doesn't show up by tomorrow, we'll send out a teletype on him. Have to wait twenty-four hours on a teletype. But then if he's anywhere in the state, we'll find him.

I'm sure you will.

Deputy Gagnon put on his fur cap. He turned to Jesse and smiled. I wouldn't bet two cents and a fish-hook on that Strongbow, Jesse.

And then the man was out the door. The boy called after him: Thanks for the bathroom.

Evening. A wind with ice in its sound soughed
through the bare trees like the rattle of skeletons. And
it swept the last of the snow out of the air. Bright stars
now glistened in one sky but not in Jesse's. Jesse's sky
was pitch-black. For he'd learned at supper what they
were planning to do with him. He'd learned it in this
way:

It started with hamburgers. The old man brought
them out and said, Dig in, boys. Jeff said please pass
the salt and Jesse did, backing up in his chair and
passing it like a quarterback. The shaker crashed
against the woodstove and scattered salt everywhere,
millions upon millions of little grains all across the
floor. A bum pass.

At which Jeff turned to his father. You see? He's
only getting worse and worse. Can't control him at all.
Only one thing you can do with a kid like that. I'll
take him down myself on Monday. Monday's when
they take regular admissions.

I guess you're right, Jeff. I been holding out too
long.

It's only natural, what with one thing and another, to keep him out. But he's just too much for one
person to handle now. You have your life to live, too.

You're right, Jeff. But I'll go down with you. I
don't want him to remember me for a skunk or something. . . .

The boy asked what the blazes they were talking
about.

Said Jeff to his father: You want to tell him?

The old man gazed at his younger son with that
sadeyed monkey face which of late made Jesse feel
the man's days were numbered. And he said: This is
important, boy. Stop fiddling with your silverware.
Kindly listen. We've been talking . . . your brother

and me . . . about you and what we can do to, well, help you. . . .

Hit the Miracle Mile tomorrow. That'd help me. Burn some rubber . . .

Boy . . .

Or maybe find Hack again . . .

I said listen. Don't interrupt. It's bad manners. Now. The old man paused and when he began to speak again his lips were trembling. He said: While you were taking your nap, we had a long talk and we both agree that you should leave home for a while, go to some other home where they can look after you a whole lot better than we can here. I'm out of the house most of the day and Jeff's not going to be around too much longer, and, well, it isn't easy for me to tell you this, boy, and I want you to know that we both love you very much and we want the best for you, and that's why we've decided you should go to Concord.

You don't love me! the boy hollered.

We do, Jesse. Believe me we do. Christ, we love you more than—more than I can ever tell you and more than you can take in right now. Later on maybe you'll understand. But right now you have to take my word for it. Concord's the best place for you . . . a lot of folks there with troubles just like yours . . . a gym . . . a lot of sports . . .

I won't go!

The decision's not up to you, I'm afraid. . . .

No need to be afraid. If you're afraid, I won't go.

Jesse, listen to me. This is for your own good. You got to see that. We just couldn't handle you anymore. Tried, but it wasn't working. Doctors would know what's wrong. Doctors would help. Please . . .

I'm well. I don't need no doctor.

You're not well, boy. Really. At Concord they might be able to give you some medicine to make you well. . . .

The old man's voice was pleading now. Jesse put all his effort into turning that voice around, away from Concord. He said: I won't go. I'll stay here and be good. Not throw any more salt. Have good manners. Tie my own shoelaces. Not laugh in church. Be a good little boy.

Then Jeff broke in: You're going if we have to drag you there. Your dad can't go on like this. He can't go on wondering what you'll try next, which little girl you'll pick for one of your stupid stunts. Can't you see you're wrecking his life?

Don't unnerstand . . .

Well, you'll fucken understand come Monday then.

Jeff, stop, the old man said. Let me talk to the boy. Now Jesse, you just keep quiet for a while. Listen. Tomorrow we'll have a nice pancake breakfast and after church we'll all ride down together to Concord. We'll go to the big King's Store and I'll buy you whatever you want. Maybe we'll even have time to see a picture or bowl candlepins. Then we'll spend the night at your Uncle Josh's and bright and early Monday morning we'll take you to your new home. Sound good?

It sounds like shit.

And so now the boy sat alone by his window. He listened to the trees creak in the wind. Someone had taken a hammer and driven a nail into his headbone and the sharp point of that nail was Concord. That someone was his loving family. They had betrayed him.

Two pinhole eyes came down the road. They

grew bigger and bigger and Jesse saw they were the headlights of Sam Pettigrew's old Ford pickup, its back window all boarded up because the glass was out and Sam never thought to replace it. The boy wished the glass was out on his own window so then he could swing through the air on his flying trapeze, landing far, far away, in Vietnam, where they wouldn't treat him like this.

Outside in the hallway his old man said to Jeff: Old Sam's on his way there now. If I don't get a move on, I'll be late again.

It was poker night at the Elks' and the old man seemed to love poker more than he loved his Jesse.

Jeff: I got to be looking out for the time myself.

The shower hissed. The smack of soap and lather. Soon Jeff's voice was a high-pitched whine and he was singing of cheap booze and cheating women, cruel of him, Jesse thought, singing at a time like this. The boy went into the bathroom and so as to talk to Jeff he stood like he was taking a leak. You'd sing? he called out.

Sure. Hank Williams sang. Anything wrong with that? came the reply from behind the curtain.

Yeah. It stinks.

Stinks? Fellow, Hank Williams is the greatest.

Screw Hank Williams. . . .

Can't. Died fifteen years ago.

With an odor of new skin Jeff stepped from the shower and reached over his brother for a towel. He dried himself, saying, Jesse, I just got one question— are you or are you not taking a piss?

I am, but it don't want to come out. . . .

Well please get out of my way. I got a hot date tonight. Have to impress her, smell good.

His brother slapped his body with various

creams and powders till he smelled fresh off the as-
sembly line. That nice. And Jesse watched and wished
his skin was like Jeff's. Brown as a berry from all that
corn weather they had in Vietnam. He compared
arms. His were pale as dishwater. Whereupon he noticed a tattoo bluely etched into his brother's biceps.
It was a heart with an arrow through it. What's that
thing say? he asked.

It doesn't say anything. It's just a heart. . . .

Cyrus Farr's got one that says *mom*. . . .

That's right.

But we ain't got a mom. . . .

I guess we don't.

So that's why yours doesn't say anything, right?

Jeff was spraying his underarms and he glanced
almost tenderly at the boy and Jesse thought his
brother might break down and tell him, You're goddamned right, soldier. Sure would be words if there
was a mom. Words that spelled her out. Any guy that
clever deserves his own home instead of Concord. But
Jeff only said: I never seen anyone take so long to piss
in my life.

I can't because of Concord. . . .

Oh c'mon Jesse. Wipe that hangdog look off your
face. It'll be all right, you'll see. They'll look after you
down there. Those people know what's what.

I'll never piss again, and it's all your fault. . . .

Christ, Jesse . . .

Yours!

Well if you can't piss, move away from the pot. I
got to use it.

And then the hangdog boy began punching his
brother with soft little jabs, no strength in him now,
the world all an aberration and a madness to him. Jeff
parried the blows easily, smiling as he did so, and

finally he bagged the boy's head with his towel. It was as though the hangdog Jesse couldn't harm a flea. He retreated to his room and dropped to his bed and hit his pillow with far stronger fists than he could muster to hit his Jeff. He hit it till he could hit it no longer. But it wasn't dead, he was. All his dreams down the drain. Where he was going, there'd be no Grace, no Vietnam.

At last Jeff, jangling his car keys, came in to say good night. It was only that. See ya later, his brother said. But the boy wanted more, as in the old days. He leaped off his bed and stopped Jeff at the door.

What is it, Jesse? I'm in a hurry. Hot date.

Tell me a story before you go.

No time . . .

Tell me about Jasper Scoggins. Just a little story. Kindly, Jeff.

All right then. You asked for it. Just to stop your yapping and set the record straight. I can tell you about Jasper Scoggins in two seconds because I made it all up. Every last word of that story was pure bullshit. Noley and me never dug up anyone. Old Jasper is probably still resting right where they buried him.

What?

Yeah, that's right. We never did pull any stunt that night. Only stole some of Hack's beer and went out and got plastered. There was no getting even, nothing.

Tears came to the boy's eyes. You truly never dug up Jasper Scoggins? His voice broke.

You heard me right.

Aw Jeff . . .

PART III
Love Song

And that night she appeared, all yellow and horrible, bobbing up and down at his window like a puppet.

He'd finished packing. Tommy gun, toy soldiers, football, sweat socks, underwear, sneakers, and a dozen pairs of shoelaces, they were all piled together into his birthday suitcase. He even tried to peel off some of his old blue wallpaper because he liked to watch the little ponies frisking on it and it'd be nice to have them frisking on the wall of his new home. But it was just too much grind for him to get that wallpaper off. Only little slivers of it came, ponyless. And so he had given up and he began to search the room to see had he forgotten any of his soldiers. He heard someone tapping on the windowpane. It was then he saw her. A putty face, wilted nose, hair like wire mesh, and her parchment fingers brown and wiggling. Those fingers gestured him towards her.

He closed his eyes. Maybe she'd be gone by the time he opened them again. The tapping continued. Slow. Measured. Like she was beating out some sort of message to him. He looked again and on that sere and shrunken face was a wide grin, wide enough to swallow him. For it was supper, he knew, that brought her here. Jesse supper.

Come, she whistled, and it seemed like all the bony trees were whistling with her. Jeff would say it was the wind and nothing more, only the wind whip-

ping down from the hills. But Jeff had lied once too
often. The boy was freed from his brother now. All he
could believe was his own eyes and they feared the
worst. Soon those eyes would be floating in the
slumgullion.

Come, she howled.

Jesse would sooner go anywhere, even to Concord, than go with her, wicked old witch, nasty old
witch. He reached into his suitcase and brought out
his tommy gun, poised it against his side and—*rat-a-
tat-tat, rat-a-tat-tat, rat-a-tat-tat!* Die, damn you, die! he
hollered. And she must have thought this a very
funny gun and him a very funny boy, for her mouth
opened wider yet, into a great cavernous laugh. Teeth
like bent nails on an old board. The boy let her have
it again. *Rat-a-tat-tat, rat-a-tat-tat, rat-a-tat-tat, rat-a-tat-
tat!* And it seemed to him that she was even shaking
her head now, as if to say, Give it up, boy, give it up.

He had to admit the gun that had killed ten thousand gooks was worthless against one dried-up old
woman. Out of his room he ran, and into the hallway.
He tried the big cypress door that led downstairs.
Locked. His loving family hadn't taken any chances.
They jailed up their Jesse. They made sure he
wouldn't do stupid things his last night home.

The boy raced from room to room in the upstairs, to his old man's room, to Jeff's room, where the
smell of after-shave lotion still lingered. And still she
was there, motioning to him from each and every
window. She knew exactly where he'd be next and
she was there first, riding with the wind, riding
against the wind, riding a great long broom. That
broom's from our own factory, was the boy's rueful
guess.

At the double window in the hallway he told her

that if she tried to bite him, he'd bite her right back
again. *Bite these!* she croaked, and with a lurid smile
she opened her cloak to reveal her shriveled leather
tits, all veins and pustules, straggling down like empty purses. They ended in flat nipples that were covered with a foul green fungus. For a moment Jesse
couldn't help gaping in a sort of dumb fascination.
He'd never seen a pair of female tits before. Except
for the ones he'd created himself.

Come to me, boy. . . .

Go back to your old mill, you!

Back in Jeff's room he hid in the closet and
begged the Almighty please to deliver him from this
witch. He begged Him on his knees there in that dark
little room, among heaps of Jeff's old shoes. Please
don't let her eat me, God. . . . But even in prayer he
could still hear her. Tapping. Cackling. Calling for
him. He switched off God. Then he yelled at the old
woman, Go fuck yourself you old witch, in a voice
that was more like a little kid's, a baby's, than his
own.

Silly little retard, she cackled. You'll never get
away from me. . . .

You ain't gonna get me, he answered her. And
despite the closed door, he flipped her the bird.

Have a bite, sonny boy, hahaha. . . .

I won't!

C'mon, take your medicine. . . .

From his closet refuge he listened to the sound of
the windowpanes stretching against the meager wood
that held them. She was going to get him now. She
was forcing the window with those long withered
dugs of hers. They were his medicine. He was her
medicine. He tripped out in a panic and in the dark
room he stumbled over Jeff's duffel bag and he fell

flat on his ass. And on his ass he prayed: God, kindly
. . . Hissed the witch: Now you're mine! Against the
window her tits grew larger yet, they grew till the boy
could easily see hundreds of cross-hatched lines, the
grisly age of the woman. Little bugs capered over her
skin.

Don't you come any closer! Jesse shouted. He felt
around the room for something to throw at her. His
hands strayed across Jeff's desk and came upon a big
round hunk of metal. The globe of the world. The
boy picked it up and flung it with all his might. Loud
shatter of glass, the globe thumping down the roof
outside, triangles of windowpane tinkling to the floor.

When he looked again, she wasn't there. Cautiously he moved toward the broken window and
peeked out. He saw only the empty night. He wondered if he'd nailed her with the globe. Hey, witch? he
whispered into the darkness. No answer. Hey silly
witch, he said, this time louder. And his voice was
greeted only by silence. Not even the wind dared
speak. You bitch of a witch! he yelled and giggled at
his own rhyme. Then he chortled in triumph, to the
barren trees, the distant mountains, the mills and the
factories, to anyone or anything with half a mind to
listen: *Dumb bitch of a witch got hit by my pitch!*

Jesse slapped his knees. Another killing! Hack
was an accident, but this one was on purpose and he
felt proud of that. The old woman wouldn't fly into
his slumberland and plague his dreams anymore. For
which he had his friend the world to thank. It was
settled in a snowdrift. He gazed down fondly at it.
The world made a nice weapon. He placed that fact in
his brainbag of useful information.

And as he stood in his brother's room with nothing between him and the chill night air, it dawned on

him that Jeff's globe had paved the way for his escape. He could make an exit through the window in much the same way it had. Concord sucked yellow snow! Concord ate horseshit with a tablespoon! He didn't have to go there now. He could simply climb out on the roof and jump down and then away with him. He recollected his old man's warning about a broken neck. But the choice between a broken neck and Concord was an easy one. He'd take the neck. Just glue it back together again.

Jesse flew back to his room and grabbed his swimsuit and stuffed it into his suitcase. He went back into the bathroom. Out of the medicine cabinet he took down the insect repellent and a tube of suntan lotion. He saw a tube of Jeff's athlete's foot ointment and he grabbed that as well. He borrowed the sunglasses from atop his brother's dresser. Into his suitcase they all went.

After donning his lumberjack cap he was ready to leave at last. He said good-bye to the creepy old Cape house of his childhood but the house didn't answer him back. Except for a few beams creaking and boards popping. Maybe that was its good-bye. Its foundation settling ever deeper as its Jesse abandoned ship. He said good-bye to the chimney and thanked it for everything.

Now the boy knocked out the window sash and the rest of the glass with it and from the gable he climbed out on the roof, suitcase in hand. For once he didn't mind the chill night air. It touched his cheeks lightly and he greeted it with a balloon of breath. The stars were out, they flashed like nails closing the lids of the sky. If only his loving family could see him now—their (haha) retard on the rooftop! His old man would shake his head and say something like, Must have leaked out the fuel tank. And he would leave it at that, for nearly all that remained to him was the diseases that cars got. But Jeff would get wicked angry. Lips all puckered like a fat hen's ass. Little muttonhead used *his* room for an escape hatch. Maybe Jeff might even cut himself a little on the broken glass. The boy wouldn't mind that. Now.

Easing himself down slantwise Jesse slipped on a loose shingle. He tried to regain his balance and found he had but one hand. The other was taken up with his suitcase. Yet instead of releasing that suitcase he grasped it tight as a rivet and soon he was toppling, soon rolling down the roof, with an avalanche of shingles trailing in his wake. He figured the gutter would break his fall but it was half-rotten and his shoulder rammed it and dislodged it. He braced himself for a broken neck. But he landed and was cuddled all around by a cottonbed of snow. Seconds later the gutter came whooshing past his head.

He was on his back in the snow. Beside him was the globe and its face was curious as to whether he had survived the fall. He had. He was alive and kicking. And the boy considered that no small miracle. He raised his eyes to the spot from which he'd begun his tumble and then felt his still firm neck. He could think of only one explanation for it. Death happened to lampreys and gooks and Hacks and witches and their kin, but seldom if ever did it happen to him. His friend the Almighty was working double time for His Jesse, making special allowances for him that He wouldn't make for, say, Jeff. No doubt about it. Jeff wouldn't have survived that fall without at least a couple of broken legs and some fractured ribs and a bloody nose. But Hero Jesse had. No telling what a person could do with God on his side.

The boy rose up and brushed the snow from his coat. He had a hot date.

Jesse's eyes were fixed on the road ahead. Not once did he look back, for it's bad luck, his old man once told him, to look back at the beginning of a trip. He had never met with any bad luck but he didn't think he would like it. And besides, look back where?

Jauntily he swung his suitcase, a lighter load than his last load, which was Hack. A trucker burned down to a pile of ashes mingling perhaps this very moment with the ashes of somebody's dead Rover. A trucker gone up in smoke and drifting over the dump and slowly over the White Mountains to whatever universe lay beyond them. Jesse aimed to reach that universe himself. He walked with the long, easy strides of his brother. His combat boots moved through the roadside slush, which seemed to say, over and over again in a quaggy voice, Hero Jesse's on the move, Hero Jesse's on the move. . . .

Up to tonight, the boy never expected to use this suitcase. His old man gave it to him for his last birthday. Silly father. He'd gone out and bought his son, who was instructed to go only as far as the river, a suitcase. Jesse thought the old man might have palled around with too many slipping and banging transmissions. Gone bufflebrained from all that oil and grease. The boy felt a gun would have been a more appropriate gift. And he knew where there was a beauty—a bazooka sitting in the Woolworth's window in Northton all shined up and ready for action. His old man said: You're growing up, boy. You don't need toys anymore. A suitcase will come in handy someday. Someday you might decide to take a trip.

At the time Jesse was content to let the matter lie.

He was grateful for the compliment. To be a grown-up was his foremost wish. And at the time he was also worried about the groundhog seeing its shadow. Six more shitfilled weeks of winter. Stupid groundhog deserved a firing squad. But now the boy knew what his old man really meant by growing up. He meant Concord. The suitcase killed two birds with one stone: a birthday present and a going-away present. Smart thinking, dad. Your son is going away, after all. He needs a suitcase for all his gear. And since he had what he needed, Jesse harbored no ill will toward his father, only that the old man's balls would drop off.

A pickup truck swung out from a side road and stopped. Fred Orem with Penny and their baby girl in pink swaddling clothes, her mouth at a milk bottle. Jesse hadn't seen the little girl before. He'd lost interest when he heard she didn't have a hunchback. Now he gazed at her. He couldn't deny that she was a cute little thing, though no hunchback. She looked cute enough to eat. But he didn't try to eat her. He was not that kind of boy. Kitchee-goo, goo, goo, he gurgled at the baby. The baby looked at him and then started to cry.

Fred peered out. Where you going? he said in a rough voice.

Looking for Hack.

With a suitcase?

Put him in it . . .

The baby was sputtering and bawling, milk dribbling down its little chin. The boy heard Penny say, Let's get moving, Fred. No use arguing with a loony. Its wheels screeched on the ice and the truck nearly hit the boy as it pulled away.

Speed demon! he shouted, smiling. Even the prospect of being run over could not dampen his high spirits. He marched on. Sang the slush: Left, right, left, right, who's that crushing me tonight? He began to meet with the telltale beer cans and bottle shards that marked the approach to the dump. Folks got excited and threw out odds and ends of their trash before they actually made it there. The boy couldn't blame them. He was fond of the dump, too.

Ahead was the entrance gate, latched shut. He lifted the stout iron bar, and the gate tottered open. He didn't bother about shutting it again. What the hell, he thought. Nothing could escape but rats and a few more rats wouldn't matter to a town like Hollinsford. A few more rats might even help out some lonely Canuck who had the hots.

Once inside he could hear them again, screech-screeching rat talk to each other. With Sam gone and the fires down, they were in their glory. They could rampage as freely as they wanted, with only a few old river cats to dispute their claim to all this ripe decay. One of these cats, a tom with huge dilated pupils, now sat beside a twisted shell of a John Deere and regarded the boy with cold scorn as he passed by. He announced to it: Jesse's the name, war's my game. . . . And had it been Puss-in-boots, he believed it would have trembled in its boots. But it was only a Hollinsford dump cat and it went *Phfffft! Phfffft!* at him. No respect.

Jesse skirted the dump furniture, bed frames and seatless chairs and old sofas, that Sam had set aside for interested parties. His lantern was the reddish glow off the garbage and he headed straight to the place where he left Hack the night before. He was keen to find out if anything remained of the remains. He hoped not. He wanted to wash his hands of the Hack affair and go on to bigger and better things.

He stepped through a sludge of rats. They shied away at his advance. They seemed to think he ate rats for breakfast. He came to what he guessed was the right pile of trash. He recognized a broken-down washer, lying on the edge of the pit. The pile had a new coating, fresh black bags split open and cans and table scraps spilling out. The chirruping rats darted in and out like they'd made a real find. That find, Jesse figured, was Hack. Or what carrion still hung to the trucker's bones. Little mouthfuls of sizzling flesh, perhaps a finger or two, a coil of intestine. Hard to beat that grub when you're a rat.

You rats doing a good job on ole Hack? the boy inquired. And from the ruckus they raised he took their answer to be yes. He clapped his hands for the creatures. His friends the rats. He vowed to forego rat in favor of barbed wire and fishhooks for his breakfast.

And then Jesse turned his attention to the Pettigrew trailer, a single yellow light glowing in it, a beacon for him. He moved toward it as to a magnet. Through Saturday's lush and teeming garbage, a dreamlike figure. Arms swaying, feet steadfast and driven, kicking aside what stood in their way. The gravel path he headed down seemed like primrose now. He walked up the cinderblock steps of the trailer and tested the door and found it unlocked. He admitted himself to the Pettigrew world. Narrow space for folks to live.

Right away there were monster noises somewhere inside. Strange shrieks and bellowings. The boy reckoned it was only the TV. He took the precaution of getting out his tommy gun anyway. Blow the bastard (if bastard there was) back to outer space. Jesse crept around the Formica table and into a living room furnished by Sam's own hand from the dump. Walls lined with old hunting calendars and pictures of kittens. Along the way he cast his eyes around for some sort of hidden chimney.

He came to the bedroom. The door lay ajar. He pushed it open to reveal Grace curled up and asleep on the bed. He was dead right—the only monsters in sight were two dinosaurs on the TV. For a moment he watched them tear and rip at each other's armored flesh, then he switched back to Grace. He stared down at the girl. She was sheathed in blue-and-white-striped gingham pajamas, her red hair bunched around her shoulders and even redder now in the light of the small room. And on her angel face was a pretty smile. Dreaming of little kitties, I'll bet, thought Jesse. His own sweet Grace. She could soften the heart of even the most crazed and rat-hungry of Canucks. The girl was of a birth unknown to him and that made her a marvel. Somehow she'd managed to come into this world without the stork's help. The bird would have circled the Pettigrew trailer for days trying to sight a chimney and at last given up and left the girl to die in some desert or frigid glacier. Jesse shook his head in amazement. The girl was a mystery. She was also lying here for his pleasure, to do with as he chose.

And he chose. First the tits. He had to make sure. He didn't want a repeat of his experience with the old witch. He didn't want to be stuck with sordid brown dugs and their fungus-ridden paps for the rest of his days. With eager fingers he began to unbutton the girl's top. Knuckles skimming the soft skin beneath. Two buttons, three. Long willowy girl. And then the last button. Breathing heavily he drew aside the gingham and looked. Two small applesized tits softly billowed up from the cloud of freckles on the girl's chest, tits stained ever so lightly with nipples no bigger than pennies. Not bad. He cupped one. It was a perfect fit.

A healthy spittle on the boy's lips. He dropped his trousers and leaped into bed with the girl. Sweet scent of sleep. Grace didn't stir. Thought Jesse: Must be real nice kitties to keep her asleep with me here. He shook her and she mumbled something about Daddy but she didn't wake up. He'd do it to her sleeping then. He couldn't hold his horses now. He was so fired up that he'd do it to her though she was dead.

He straightened out her body, stretched apart her legs, then commenced heaving around on top of her.

And who could say whether it was the boy's hands tugging at her pajama bottoms or his teeth at her breasts or his cock pressing hard into her thigh that finally woke Grace up? But wake up she did, with big languid eyes, and when she saw the fervid boy astraddle her, instead of screaming or pushing him off, she only yawned.

Hi Grace, Jesse gasped.

Daddy don't like you here . . . that tickles. . . .

. . . t'hell with Daddy . . .

And soon he had her bottoms down to her knees, not without her squirming to help him, though she seemed not to know or care what he was planning to do with her. And he caught a glimpse of the little pink tuftlet of hair that would be her pussy, funny name for it, Jesse thought, it had neither claws nor a tail, thank God. Looking down he saw half-hidden by this hair a slit more or less like Margaret's. He went all eyeballs and mouth. No one needed to tell him that this was the gateway to love.

The girl cried: Ouch Jesse . . . that's rough stuff.

. . . But at his bidding her thighs spread open bone-lessly.

His breath came in shorter, quicker spurts. It was a tight squeeze but he made it at last. Paydirt. *Accch! That hurts!* The boy was miles and miles inside his Grace, exploding away like mad, bombs like flowers, *bamm! bamm! bamm!,* a happy bombardier loose in the land he loved. He blew out his tubes there, in the warm grass. Later he would think about reloading. As for now, he began eating more far more than his ration of freckles. Jesse slurping at those little apples with his favorite animal noises and—*Ouch! You bite!*

The girl was put out. She told him that this rough new game made her bleed.

Bleed where?

Where I go to the bathroom . . .

Well, it don't make me bleed. . . .

Ick. It's all over the sheet.

By now Jesse had grown accustomed to this kind of bleeding. He decided that must be what it was all about. This thing called love. He said: Has to bleed for it to be right.

Grace said she didn't like it nearly as much as jump rope. She tried to wiggle out from under the boy.

Jesse: You gotta learn to like it. Because it's love. It's a boy's game. Girls got their own games. . . .

It's what grown-ups do at night. . . .

. . . plus girls' games don't hurt . . .

Somebody's got to get hurt. . . .

You ever played *Just like me* before?

Jesse said he didn't like games that had a lot of rules.

Oh this one's easy. Just say *Just like me* every time I stop, and I'll tell you a real good story. All right?

Okeydokey.

I went into this big old scary house. . . .

Just like me.

Right. That's good. And I went up the stairs. . . .

Just like me.

I walked down a dark old hall. . . .

Just like me.

I went into a scary little room. . . .

Just like me.

I looked out the window. . . .

Just like me.

And I saw a monkey. . . .

Just like me.

Just like *you! Ha ha ha* . . .

Jesse laughed, too. Part of his laugh was directed at himself, a monkey. The other part came from how glad he was to be here with Grace. He could really talk to this girl. She wasn't like some of the others. She was special.

As on the TV a group of cave people did a kind of square dance around the dead dinosaurs and then *Monster Theater* was over.

. . . arraigned before District Court in Manchester on second-degree homicide charges. And now this final note before the weather. Franconia's Chester Folensbee is a water diviner who recently got a phone call from Saudi Arabia. Seems this sheikh out there heard about Chester and wanted him to . . .

The boy switched it off and returned to bed. Still naked, they'd spent the last hour watching TV. And now Jesse was ready to ask Grace the big question. He had to know her answer to this question. He said: You wanna run away to Nam with me, huh, Grace?

Her eyes blinked. *Where* you going?

Vietnam. You come with me. . . .

Right now? Right this very moment? I don't know. . . .

You'll love it. Honest. They don't got winter there. Just summer every day. And nice beaches . . .

But ain't that where they been fighting? Vietnam?

Jesse was pleased as punch. He hadn't expected her to know so much about it. Yeah, he said. Fighting's why I'm headed there. Gonna kill me some gooks and take in those rays. . . .

Kill?

It's my business, the boy said.

Well, I'm just a girl and I never killed anyone before, pouted Grace.

Jesse told her it was easy once you got the hang of it. But since you're just a girl, he added, all you got to do is lie on the beach. Us guys'll do the rest. . . .

The rest of what?

You know. Defend the country. Keep those yellowskins out of New Hampshire.

Geez, Jesse. Daddy wouldn't want me to run away.

That simp. Never been to Vietnam himself, I bet.

Daddy doesn't like me to go anywhere. Keeps me all cooped up. I don't get out ever at all except for school.

School's for dummies that don't know nothing, the boy said.

I never been anywhere before, the girl went on. Only to Northton and Bethel and once to Laconia to see my auntie. But that doesn't count. She was sick and dying. Fell on the ice and broke her hip and everything . . .

No sick and dying in Vietnam . . .

I never been anywhere . . . In girlish annoyance she

smacked her pink knee with her palm. She was coming around to his way of thinking. He said: Run away
with me then. See things . . .

What things?

Things like you never seen before. Jungles and
high mountains. Choppers. Heads popped like melons . . .

But daddy . . .

Like to shoot that mother . . .

Never get a chance. He'll take his gun to you
first. Find you here playing with me and he'll shoot
you right between the eyes, silly.

Then I'll shoot him right back again, Jesse said.
Shoot him *in* the eyes . . .

I don't even know where Vietnam's at. . . .

Don't know either. Can't be far, though.

As far as Manchester?

The boy scratched his head to indicate thought.
Then he informed his Grace that he expected Vietnam was somewhere around California.

California! she exclaimed. That's where my
mommy lives. Can we go and see her? Ain't never
seen my mommy before.

Dunno. Vietnam might come before California. . . .

Don't be mean Jesse. . . .

. . . and anyway mommies are for sissies, the boy
stated. For he didn't want the trip messed up by a
mommy or a sister or whatever Grace happened to
call her. He was dead certain the girl would be taken
away from him if they started meeting members of
her family. Mommies, especially, were trouble. He
gathered as much from listening to the kids.

Grace: Then I just won't go. Not unless I get to
see my mommy.

To this Jesse replied: Sun's better than any

mommy. That's Vietnam for you. Sun. Girls love it. They sit around all day taking the rays. It's so hot, all you need is a bikini. . . .

Don't even got a bikini.

And Jesse reached into his pants and brought out all damp and moldy the thing he'd found that afternoon by the river. He figured it might help convince her. Smiling he gave it to the girl. Ugh! she exclaimed. Throw it away!

But it's a bikini. . . .

Crazy. It's just a smelly old bra. Throw it away. . . .

The boy did as he was told. Grace was more stubborn than he expected. He decided anything to get her ass on the road. So told her: All right. California first. We'll go and see your stupid mommy.

Honest?

Honest Injun . . .

Cross your heart and hope to die?

Cross my heart and hope to die, Jesse said. But behind his back he crossed his fingers. They uncrossed his heart and caused him not to die. He did it just to be on the safe side. He knew God wouldn't let him die, but God in His nightly rounds mightn't be looking into the Pettigrew trailer. God might be asleep or trying to sleep or for that matter fondling tits somewhere. Nice round apple tits, with pinkeyed nipples, to do with as He chose.

Grace was giggling and pointing.

The boy looked down. Christmas, he'd grown a baseball bat again! Crash that ball out of sight, crash the living daylights out of it! He shoved the girl back on the bed and again climbed on top of her, but she rolled out from under him. She said she wasn't in the mood. She said she was still sore from last time.

S'posed to be sore, he told her.

Then let's not play that icky game again, OK?

The prospect of a life without love did not appeal to the boy. It's my favorite game, he yelled, drumming his fists against the bed.

And Grace knew she had made him unhappy. She patted him on his bare back, merciful little fingers, and told him maybe she could learn to like it. Maybe if they didn't play it for a while. Maybe wait till they got to Nam . . .

He brightened. You mean you're going?

I was going all along, silly. Don't you understand girls?

And there on her lips Jesse gave his Grace the first kiss he had ever given to anyone outside his own family. He'd seen them kiss like that in old movies.

As soon as she began to pack, Jesse learned why they called her slow. The girl got bogged down after her toothbrush. She had only three dresses and she couldn't decide which one to take. She stood by her dresser and stared at the open drawer and little jeweled tears slithered down her cheeks.

At first Jesse thought her shilly-shallying quite funny. Yellow's a good color for Nam, he snickered. He told her to forget about dresses and just take some jeans and a shirt and they'd pick up a bikini somewhere along the way. But she went on crying and said she needed something nice to wear. Just like a girl, Jesse felt. Worrying about clothes in the middle of a war.

The boy grew impatient. He paced the floor and then began to rummage inside the cupboards of the Pettigrew trailer. In search of such bric-a-brac as Vietnam required. He scooped up a whole arsenal of meat forks, corkscrews, can openers, skewers, and knives of varying sizes and shapes. He only wished Grace and her father ate with bayonets. But in place of a bayonet he might be able to get by with silverware. Matches. He took them as well. He might want to set fire to a thatched roof somewhere.

He returned to the bedroom carrying his plunder. Grace was in a ruffly white dress with a big bow at the waist. She was curtsying in front of the mirror. Think this'll be OK? she asked the boy. Bikini's nicer, he said. And dropped the kitchen utensils with a clatter in his suitcase. The girl watched. Stealing our silver? she smiled.

Hah. A lot you know. These make good weapons.

Looks like you're stealing our silver to me.

It's wrong to steal, Jesse told her.

The girl reached into his suitcase and picked up his tommy gun. He wrenched it away from her. He didn't like anyone, even his girl friend, touching his gun. She might throw some mechanism out of kilter.

Daddy's got one that's bigger, said Grace a little sulkily.

I seen his. Mine's better. Killed almost ten thousand gooks with it.

Daddy uses his just on rats.

See? Mine is made to kill people. Just like with all good guns . . .

Daddy hardly uses his on people at all.

Figures, Jesse said. And the thought went through his mind that he could use another gun, even if it was only a .22 rimfire. He could shoot the smaller varmint-type gooks with it. Another gun would give his trusty tommy an occasional rest. Or he could pack them both at the same time. Hero Jesse the One-Man Army, that's what they'd call him. He came at you

with a gun in each hand, and steak knives and forks
and can openers dangling from his artillery belt.

And so he decided to add Sam's rat rifle to his
swelling arsenal. Where's this gun at? he asked Grace.

Locked up.

Locked up where?

Above the bathroom. But I don't got a key.

Never you mind a key. Just hurry up and I'll do
the rest.

The bathroom was a narrow door wedged into
the kitchen. Jesse grabbed a reupholstered chair. The
whole world could be a weapon with the right man
behind it. He'd knocked off Hack and the old witch,
and now it was time fòr the Pettigrew bathroom to
bite the dust. He crashed the chair into the reedy
planking above the door. Then he climbed onto the
chemical toilet and cleared away the splintered wood
and poked his hand through the opening. He felt
chilly metal of the sort that would outlast every man
jack one of them, as Sam would say. Gently he took
the rifle down and hugged it to his chest. Hugged it all
the more lovesomely for it looked like it'd been
abused. The stock and forearm were battered and
wormeaten, the bluing was gone, and the sling swivel
was rusty as an old nail. Sam been nasty to you? he
said, petting the rifle.

The boy tried firing his new weapon *bchhhhhh!*
with a guttural blast from the back of his throat. Not
bad. Nice action. Power. He fired again *bchhhrrrr!*
Bchhhrrrr! The kick damn near knocked him over. He
was liking this gun more and more. He ran his fingers
along its sleek metal barrel. He had to admit that his
own tommy gun was like a toy compared to this
baby. You gonna be a load of fun, he said to it. He
aimed, fired again. *Bchhhrrrrr!* The whizzing shell

stopped a water buffalo dead in its tracks. One hell-uva big varmint.

How long he stood there on the toilet fingering his new gun he couldn't have said. And time to the deathless boy was of no account anyway. But he was brought back to his senses when he heard Sam's pickup rumble distantly across the dump toward home. He leaped down and ran back to the bedroom. Let's go! he hollered. Your daddy's comin'!

His only answer came from the TV: a little old lady trying to sell a meat grinder. Grace was fast asleep again. She was wearing a sailor blouse and nothing else. He tugged at her but she only giggled and rolled over. He guessed she was with those stupid kitties again. It'd be easier to bleed a turnip than to get her away from them now.

What to do? Sam would find him here and Grace's pink nubbins would be staring the man in the face. Sam would know what happened. And the dumpkeeper did not seem to be the type of person who'd take kindly to love. He might kill or maim to stop it from happening again. Jesse dashed back and forth from one end of the trailer to the other. He asked the calendars, the swing couch, the refinished furniture, the hot plate, and the icebox what to do. The icebox said to use another milk bottle. Toma-hawk the man back to the Elks. A frantic search turned up no milk bottle, only cans of beer and some-thing in a bowl that looked and smelled like dead earthworms. Leftover spaghetti. Hardly much of a weapon. The boy kicked the dumb icebox.

For a moment he fiddled with the door. He wasn't very clever with doors. He could smash them, but this one needed not smashing so much as locking. Little chance to master it now. The boy heard Sam's truck pull up behind the trailer and a grating of gears and the motor die with a spastic sucking noise. The door slam. Steps on the gravel. Crunch, crunch, crunch. Jesse's last resort was to blockade the door with the swing couch. He started pushing. It was only then that he was reminded of the rifle. In his hurry he'd thrown it on the swing couch. A rifle might very well prove to be a better weapon than a milk bottle.

The steps halted. Grace, that ·you? . . . *Grace!* called a worry-voiced Sam. All that fiddling and shuffling inside must have told him something was wrong.

The boy shouted: No, it's me! He flung open the door and stood blocking the entrance with the rifle in both his hands, a prideful smirk on his face.

Jesse . . . what the hell . . . what's happened to Grace? Eyes nearly leaping out of their sockets.

I'm her father now, haha. . . .

You crazy? Gimme that. . . .

Jesse swung the gun away from the man. Mine now, he said.

How long you been here. . . .

. . . forever and ever . . .

You done anything to Grace, I'll . . .

You'll *what.* Next Jesse pointed the barrel directly at the man. He would never kill anyone with whom he so enjoyed shooting the shit as Sam Pettigrew. However, he did want to give Sam a good fright after last night's rude treatment. The boy went *bchhhrrrrr! Bchhhrrrrr!* Dance, he said. Dance you mother. . . . On the TV he'd often heard men with guns say that, though for what reason he never knew.

Sam seemed to have no intention of dancing. He moved in closer and squinted up at Jesse. If you even touched a hair on my little girl's head . . .

You're not dancing!

The man's lank and corded hands pounced on the rifle, slid down and off the barrel. They pounced again and this time held on. Old as Sam was, he was strong as sin. *You gimme that, boy. Just you gimme that gun. . . .* Jesse said over his dead body. And there followed a tug of war over the rifle, with Jesse pulling it toward him and Sam yanking it away and at the same time trying to sneak past the boy into the trailer. Jesse thought it all a kind of offbeat fun. He also thought Sam would make good his promise to kill him if he ever got hold of the gun. The boy was determined not to let him. He flailed out at the man with his combat boots. But nothing drove the dumpkeeper off. As he yanked, Sam's hands crept up to where the boy's hands were.

You lemme have that. . . .

No, it's mine . . . need it for my war. . . .

Now-w-w . . . And the man gave his strongest heave yet. The barrel point went into the soft flesh of his gut.

A soft click. Then the trigger seemed to pull back of its own accord with Jesse's finger on it. The boy heard a soft muffled blast, from where he could hardly tell. Sam gasped, his body shuddered. And he lurched back down the cinderblock steps, muttering, Damn, pressed the safety catch. . . .

That's a good dance, Jesse observed. For in his innocence he didn't even realize the gun had gone off. The dull noise he'd heard was not a sound platoons could live by. It was more like an old man farting, Sam farting, in fact. It certainly wasn't him.

Safety catch . . .

Slugs, grinned the boy.

And now Sam was plopped down in a mire of slush and gravel. His legs twinged. He seemed to have

folded up. He burbled: Think it hit . . . the spine . . .
can't hardly move. . . .

Thought Jesse: Must have been one helluva fart.

. . . doctor . . .

You sick? asked Jesse.

Goddamn it . . . get me a doctor. . . .

I make you sick, Mr. Pettigrew?

. . . can't move none . . .

Throw up. You'll feel better.

. . . hollow pointer . . . tore through . . . gut . . .

You ate too much beans, I bet, the boy said. He
was of the opinion that Sam had been felled by a bad
stomach ache. He felt it might be something the man
ate. Perhaps Sam got his food as well as his furniture
from the dump. Scooped out what was left from old
bean cans. The boy didn't think that would be too
healthy. He told Sam that. He felt perhaps not enough
steak and mashed potatoes found their way to the
Pettigrew dinner table. He told Sam that, too.

. . . doctor . . .

I'm beat, Mr. Pettigrew.

. . . please . . .

Jesse yawned. He knew it was bad manners, but
he'd had a big day and he was too worn out to last
much longer. Nor did he believe they could hit the
Vietnam trail tonight. He'd have to wake Grace again.
Help her pack. Drag themselves out of the trailer.
Weary feet dragged down by the road. All he wanted
to do now was lie down next to his Grace and join her
in slumberland. Dream of tanks and M-60s and
touchdowns. Tomorrow was another day. They'd
greet the dawn with their bootsteps.

Of course he couldn't forget about the dumpkeeper. Now he regarded the quiet shape on the
ground. He kicked that shape in the side to make sure

Sam wasn't playing possum. The man gave a weak moan and that was it. No possum. He did not appear to be in a killing mood. He looked too sick to be doing any killing, so he did. Jesse felt the man should be inside in bed, though that was where he himself would be, with Grace. The boy looked toward the frayed brown mattress that lay in the snow a few feet away. It was the same mattress that Sam shot just the night before, to show off his might.

Jesse lugging Sam Pettigrew as he'd lugged Hack, under the arms, movie-style. He met with no resistance from the man's rubbery body.

The mattress gave off a faint reek of decay, as of dead birds or small mouse bodies buried inside it. Sam, living in a dump, was no doubt used to that. The boy raised him up and rolled him onto the mattress. You'll be all right here, he said. He touched the man lightly on his aching tummy. When he drew away his hand, he found a dark speck of blood on it. The blood came from a flysized hole in the dumpkeeper's tummy. Jesse had never heard of a stomach ache bleeding before. It only proved to him how bad Sam's must be. Poor bastard, he said.

No one could call him unthinking. From the trailer he brought out an old gray army blanket that was being used as a rug and he pulled it over Sam and tucked him in for the night. He told the man it'd be like camping out. Fun to sleep out under the stars. Some would give their eyeteeth to be here with him.

. . . oh dear God . . .

That's right, Mr. Pettigrew. It's time to say your prayers.

Inside the trailer Jesse was ready to hit the hay himself. Then he recalled that his old man once told him that the best thing for a person sick to his stomach was to eat some food. And tired as the boy was, he still went to the icebox and took out the spaghetti, stuck a fork in it, and carried it with a can of beer back to the sick man. He said: You eat that and you'll feel better. It seemed some rats wanted to feel better, too. He noticed a few of them skulking around, darting under the trailer, naked scaly tails. He hoped they wouldn't try to steal Sam's spaghetti. They might mistake it for worms, a food dear to their rathearts. But he was too dogtired (poor bastard himself) to worry about that now. Let Sam fight it out with the rats over the bowl of spaghetti. At least the man had his beer. See ya in the morning, the boy yawned.

Jesse brought the rifle into the bedroom with him. On the off chance that Sam came calling during the night. He passed by the TV, which was a blank silver screen scraping with static. Without bothering to turn it off he lay down in bed fully clothed, Grace on one side of him, his rifle on the other. They slept.

PART IV
Flight

Morning bright as birdsong. The drip-drip-drip of snow melting off the Pettigrew trailer. The sky poured into the little room and lit it up like a lamp. Light lay across the curled-up girl, the barely awakened boy now regarding that thin body now all ablaze.

All his thoughts brought him back to Grace's mystery. No one needed to tell him that he and the girl were made for each other. They were creatures of a single feather. He was safeguarded by the Almighty and she was born like no one else, perhaps dropped storkless to earth by the Almighty Himself. In Vietnam they'd make the perfect couple.

On the TV a big bad wolf was chasing a silly duck across a waste of cactus and ox skulls. Jesse grabbed the .22 and aimed it at both of them. *Bang! Bang!* And when the girl blinked open her big round deereyes, he told her: Shot 'em both deader'n doornails. . . .

Silly. They're not even alive. . . .

Not now they ain't.

I'm hungry, she replied. She rose to her haunches and stretched and then lay down again propped up by her elbows and gazed at the TV. Small carefree ass addressing the day. Looking at the girl Jesse quickly became hungry himself. His first instinct was to wait for somebody to make breakfast and bring it in to him. There was no one to do that here. Here in the

Pettigrew trailer he could be waiting till the end of the world and he still wouldn't get any breakfast. He didn't want to wait that long so he slipped out of bed and clomped into the kitchen.

The open icebox door reminded him of Sam. He hadn't heard a peep out of the dumpkeeper this morning. He guessed the man had spent a quiet night under the stars. He decided to check up on him anyway.

Outside a ground fog wisped up from pools of water and melting snow. Through the haze the boy thought he saw a weird grin on Sam's face. And he wondered what was so funny. He found out soon enough. The spaghetti was gone. So was half of Sam's face. The rats had gnawed large chunks from it during the night and left behind a hash of congealed blood with bits of pale bone peering through. Golden-brown rags of muscle with the texture of uncooked meat. Jellylike eyes, popped, half-nibbled. A whitish matter (the brain?) seeping from a ratchewed ear. A skeleton mouth was the man's grin. His silken chin whiskers glistened in the sun.

Poor Sam! Dead as mutton. And Jesse had no doubt as to why the rats did him in. The dumpkeeper had killed far too many of them over the years. Whole families of rats bumped off by his .22. They staged this night attack because they couldn't take it any longer. It was as simple as that. The boy felt he might have done the same thing, in their place. None-theless he was a little sad walking back to the trailer. Sam was one of a kind. The only father ever to be grandfather to his daughter.

Back inside he found Grace eagerly munching a glazed doughnut. She offered him one and he took it.

He stuffed the whole thing into his mouth before starting to chew and as his jaws worked so did his mind. He decided it wouldn't be a good idea to tell the girl about Sam's mishap. A dead daddy might be bad for her morale. A dead daddy might hold up the trip. Grace would want to bring in Reverend to mutter a few words about Eternal Rewards. Christmas, she mightn't even want to spread her legs for her Jesse! Keep them clamped shut in honor of her daddy's death.

He watched the girl load cans of bologna and beans (watch out for those beans, he told himself) into her suitcase. For the road, she told him. Clever of her to think of food. Jesse saw a jar of maple syrup and he loaded that as well.

Your daddy never came back, the boy lied. He hoped she hadn't seen the pickup parked behind the trailer.

She hadn't seen it. She said: Good for us . . . right?

Yeah. He didn't murder us.

Bet he spent the night at the Elks again.

I bet that's what he did.

Once Grace had combed her hair, they were ready to leave. And Jesse told her: You gotta close your eyes now. Bad luck to look back at the beginning of a trip.

What about you? Who'll see for us?

Already begun my trip. Eyes closed already. No need to do it again.

Jesse with the rifle under his arm led the unseeing girl past her father's body and piles of debris and all the rot and mangled machinery that had once been her slender life. It was not until they reached the

wrecked cars lying at the outskirts of the dump that
the boy told his Grace to open her eyes. He let go of
her hand, sweet girl.

That means it'll be a lucky trip, huh? she said.

Luckier than shit, Jesse smiled.

Sunday morning meant no traffic. Folks were either in church or sleeping it off. Hollinsford and en-
virons laid low by prayer and hangovers. Not these
two. What could stop them now? They moved while
others slept. Full of buckram they went down the
road with lively steps and a song in their hearts. They
sang, Great green globs of greasy grimy gopher guts.
. . . They sang it over and over again for it was Jesse's
favorite road song. It made him think of enemy innards such as he would soon have the pleasure of
seeing for himself. The girl also seemed to like it
though she said she didn't know too much about the
enemy. She had never seen a gopher entire, much less
its guts spilling out great and greeny. Her daddy always kept her locked away from them.

They would have been holding hands were they
not holding so much else. The girl had her suitcase
and Jesse had his suitcase and gun, which he held like
a hand, his fingers wrapped tightly around the trigger
guard. He said: I like you more than my Tommy. . . .

What? said Grace.

I was talking to the gun. . . .

How they'd get to Vietnam, the boy didn't have a
clue. And he didn't crave a clue. He'd manage. Didn't
his old man say it was a small world? Jesse himself
guessed the world was more or less the same size as it
appeared on a TV program. And thus he suspected
that Vietnam lay only beyond the White Mountains,

in the same direction as the beach. About distances he knew little, could care less, to hell with them. He was impelled by some divine energy that worked not with maps or clues, but on instinct deep as bone, old as rock. If bats could find their caves or salmon spawn, he could find Vietnam.

For her part the girl only seemed to want California and her mommy.

Never seen her, why want her? Jesse asked.

Oh I wanna see Disneyland, too. . . .

Disneyland's for kids. . . .

Ahead was a rise and then a gulch at the bottom of which were nestled the smokestacks of Hollinsford. Both of them stopped. They seemed to have forgotten all about the town. Now it was blocking their way. A gray monster on crouched reptile legs.

We can't go that way, said Grace.

The boy shaded his eyes against the sun. The sun was the beach and Vietnam and at the moment that sun was hovering over Starkey's Hill. A four-wheel-drive track creased the hill, weaving ever upward and vanishing beyond a clump of hemlocks. All the voices of his friend the great out-of-doors whispered in his ear to take that track. They whispered all together in one chiming chorus. The piny woods whispered it, the long azure sky, even a dead bushytail crushed flat and mummified there by the roadside. The bald white head of Mount Washington knew all about Jesse's mission and it seemed to nod in his direction. Overhead whisked a pair of crows. Nam, Nam, they cried, Follow that track!

Who would not have taken this advice? Jesse pointed his Grace at the hill.

Said the girl: You wanna go mountain climbing?

Well, it's the right way. . . .

Geez, you just about need snowshoes. The girl walked back to the road.

I'm the man here, Jesse said. I'm the one s'posed to do the thinking.

Well, pooh to you!

C'mon, Grace. We don't got all day.

Let's take a highway instead. There're loads of them around. The girl stood there unmoving, her face lit up by the thought of highways. Stubborn little thing, thought Jesse. Again he commanded her to start on up the hill. That'll be our highway, he told her.

You're gonna get us lost, she said.

Not me. I'm a platoon leader. Know this country like the back of my hand.

Oughter have a map . . .

The notion of a map was an insult to the whole platoon. Jesse said: Don't need a map to do what's right.

You got the squirts, Jesse. . . .

Shut up! he yelled. And he swiped his Grace across the mouth. It was a swipe designed to show the girl who was boss rather than hurt her. Perhaps she (who didn't seem to hear all those woodland voices) would understand fist language. No less an authority than Raymond Perkins once told Jesse that girls needed to be hit. It kept them in line. They wanted to be hit, but sometimes they were afraid to ask.

Grace got the message. She cringed back. She seemed to be no newcomer to swipes. She only needed this one to set her on the right track. Jesse smiled as she started walking up the hill. That's more like it, he said. His Grace knew who wore the pants on this trip. He followed close behind her. In case she should slip, he'd save her from a nasty fall. The boy was a gentleman.

As hills went, Starkey's Hill wasn't much. An Indian chief was supposed to have jumped to his death from the top. Nowadays kids necked up there if their parents wouldn't let them neck at home. Old folks from Massachusetts climbed the hill. And with his brother Jesse himself had even climbed it. That was a summer in times long past. The boy could recall a sweet plant reek in the air. Pine breath. Hushed and mazy afternoon. The brothers scrabbled up to the lookout in less time, it seemed, than it usually took Jesse to tie his shoelaces in the morning. The boy asked about the tower. Jeff told him: It's to spot forest fires. Only there aren't enough around here so they put the ranger somewhere else. That wasn't very nice, said Jesse. He was disappointed. He thought of forest rangers as a mountainy breed of cop. He lit match after match and flung them from the tower in hopes of starting a fire and bringing back one of the rangers. At last Jeff saw him at it, slapped his hands lightly and took away the matches. Jeff said: You don't want to do that, Jesse. What if you started a forest fire? But that's what I'm trying to do, the boy informed his brother.

The track was pressed hard as concrete by snow-machines. Their grid marks made good footholds. Jesse and the girl moved up the hill using the herringbone steps of skiers. The girl was as surefooted as a goat. You oughter be glad you got on your boots, the boy grinned, and not your dress-up shoes. Grace grumped back that she was glad. As was Jesse himself. Humming the gopher tune he wielded his rifle like a walking stick, but with its barrel down. He was no dummy. He didn't want to blow out his brains now that he had gotten this far.

Two lone specks on an altar of ice. Anyone who saw them from a distance would have said they were early skiers out for a morning on the slopes. Except that they bore the strange prop of suitcases. Skiers never took suitcases. Those suitcases would have made that anyone wonder. They made the boy himself wonder. He felt Kennebeckers would have been more appropriate. Or soldiers' camp bags, with mess kits dangling from them. And for himself, gray army fatigues. Yet it wasn't his fault he was outfitted so poorly. He'd had no time to pay a visit to the quartermaster. No time even to see the draft board.

Soon the slope started to become steeper. Rocks like knife blades rising from the snow, sharp edges all jagged and at times showing the sunny gleam of steel, at other times red rust. Trickles of water ran alongside the track. An old downed hemlock lay in a nearby gully. Can't we stop and rest here? Grace asked.

Nah. Wait till the top. Don't got much further.

I'm sort of pooped. . . .

Wait to be pooped. Those are my orders. Your CO speaking.

Jesse, you getting to be just like my daddy.

Ain't never tended a dump in my life, the boy told her.

They turned a bend which passed near the edge and from that spot they saw Hollinsford resting below them like a deserted village. My platoon's gonna kill a helluva lot more than water buffaloes, Jesse said.

I know. Gophers.

Yellowskins, you silly.

I thought you was after gophers. . . .

Hell don't you pay any attention to the TV at all?

Pay more attention than you, Mr. Smarty.

Hell you do!

Presently the lookout tower, creaking in the wind, loomed above them. By now even Jesse was a little breathless. He wasn't really accustomed to these altitudes. The flat ground was more his territory for it allowed him to walk like a king. Huffing he reached the top. He stood amid a skein of snowmachine trails, each snaking off in a different direction. Finally the girl came into view and she slouched toward him as though her suitcase were packed with cinderblocks. She said something he couldn't hear owing to the wind. What? he hollered. I said it's windy! she yelled back. And right then a big gust of wind slammed off the boy's lumberjack cap and sent it whistling across the snow. He bent to pick it up and the wind nearly picked him up and flung him on the snow, too. Geez, he yelled, let's hit the tower!

Quick feet clattering on metal stairs as below the town of Hollinsford appeared again. Jesse hoisted up the trapdoor and they entered the lookout chamber, a midden of broken glass, rags, rubbers, wadded newspapers, and half-frozen shit. Canuck housekeeping, thought the boy.

Ugh! Grace exclaimed. This place stinks.

Oughter remind you of home, said Jesse.

Reminds me of an outhouse. . . .

You rather be outside blown all the way to Boston?

Rather be with my mommy.

By now the boy had worked up quite an appetite. He patted his tummy. You can't eat no mommy, he said. And he began to forage through Grace's suitcase in search of something he could eat. No wonder she was so tired lugging it—it was a whole larder of cans.

He drew out some bologna. Raymond says bologna makes a man want to screw, he winked.

You're not gonna eat here?

Sure. Have a picnic.

The girl made a face. She seemed to find the place a little unsavory for a picnic. Off she moved to one of the few unbroken windows. She looked none too happy. Weary hangdog girl, gazing down on tiny Hollinsford. One hundred mouse houses. Insect cars rolling down the streets. The river bent around the town as though trying to avoid it. The wind, in wobbling the tower, wobbled the town.

Armed with the can of bologna, Jesse walked over to his girl. He wanted to impress her with his strength so he sought to open the can with no tool but his own workaday hands. First he tried to pull the sides loose, then he pressed and squeezed at the seams. He tried his teeth but nothing worked. Grace told him to use the can opener, silly. He retrieved it from amongst his weaponry and ran the triangular point along the edge, pushing hard as he went. That didn't work, either.

The girl said: You dummy. You've gone and brought the wrong kind of opener.

There ain't no wrong kind. . . .

There sure is. This one's for beer cans.

He replied: I don't drink beer. Milk's my brew. But he knew he had done wrong. He stood there sheepishly. As Reverend always said, who among us is not without fault? The truth of these words stung him.

Grace was searching for the right opener. She jangled a wealth of pronged and pointed kitchen utensils using which Jesse would do battle. You got everything here but the kitchen sink, she declared. That too, the boy said. He hoped by this joke that she'd see his ability. Except for can openers he was as clever as the next person. Yet she didn't seem to be convinced. Guess we ain't gonna eat, she said.

In his frustration he threw the can against the wall. He picked it up from a wadded newspaper and threw it again. A few inches higher and he would have hurled it clear out the window. He brought out a steak knife. Again and again he stabbed the can. You sonofabitch! he swore at it. He was not at all pleased that his girl had called him a dummy. He took it out on the bologna, striping the can with knife wounds. Little morsels of meat began to ooze out of the slits. And this gave him an idea. He inserted the knife under one of the slits and twisted and a flap of metal came up. Twice again he inserted it and tugged back on the metal. Soon he'd made a gaping hole in the top. Jellied pink meat ready for the taking. He was no dummy now. With his fingers he scooped out a wad of bologna and offered it to the girl, as if to say, Strongarmed Jesse's the best opener on the market. Grace refused it with a shake of her head. Thought the boy: She doesn't care for all that frozen shit with her food. As for himself, he was not one to require a spread in the Ritz.

Jesse used the skewer as a makeshift fork. He thrust chunk after chunk of finetasting grub into his mouth. He chewed with his favorite animal noises and ate until there was no more. And then he patted his stomach contentedly. Raymond Perkins was right. The bologna did make him want to screw. He was about to attack another can when the girl said, I think I see my daddy down there.

Where?

Down by the church. He just came out of the church.

Let me see.

Looks like an ant from up here . . .

The boy drew closer as though to search out Grace's daddy from among the other ant people. He sniffed at her hair and coat, inhaled her skin. Sweet girl smell in the midst of all this mountainy filth. He said: Yeah, I can see him, too. Heading home . . .

Boy will he be mad when he gets there!

Jesse put his arm around the girl's waist and wrenched her towards him. His hands shoved at the buttons of her coat and blouse. She strained away. Don't feel like playing now, she said to him. She might have been talking to a block of wood or a stone. A stone which slurped at her mouth and throttled her breasts. Don't, Jesse! she exclaimed, pulling away again, trying to close her coat.

But he wouldn't have been Jesse had he let her escape. He backed the girl against the broad windowsill. Facing her, he could also see white nature beam a blessing on him. He decided to do it standing up this time. Never did it standing up before. The condition of the floor helped him decide. It was not the softest or the cleanest of beds. And he didn't want his girl to be uncomfortable.

Belly to belly he rubbed against her in order to rev up his motor. Weakly she shook her head. Soft fists beating on his shoulders. Her eyes pleased him. Fearful.

Ain't you glad you came now? Jesse grinned. And he kept on grinning as he slid down her panties and peered at her pussy. The girl complained it was still sore, but it looked all right to him. Who would have thought a rosethatch like hers could be found in a ugly place like Hollinsford? He grunted for sheer pleasure and unzipped his jeans.

His entire body became a sledgehammer whacking away at a nail. Grace cried Stop! but that only made the boy thrust at her harder. Soon she couldn't be heard at all. Her voice was drowned out by a kind of loud whirring. Jesse thought it might be a snow-machine but what snowmachine flies through the sky? What snowmachine could roar like that? The tower gave him a clear view of what happened next. Suddenly out of the mountains came a great Chinook chopper, its twin rotors twirling so fast they were almost invisible. For a moment it appeared to hover peaceably over the town of Hollinsford, suspended like a hawk regarding its prey. Then it attacked that prey. With a loud roar it dropped straight down and started dumping its load of M-79 rounds and canisters of napalm.

And down on the church the bombs fell *keerash! keerash!* They fell on the broom-handle factory, the pizza palace, the post office, Perley Dimick the stone-mason's yard, Thibodeaux's Market, and on the Heritage Spa a big one. *Keerash! Boom!* There wasn't a dud in the lot. Fires burned away at the town like it was made of straw. Too much dry timber caused the flames to hurtle from house to house. Old frame houses snap, crackle, and popping. Caterpillars of flame wriggling across a hundred hardwood floors. Blazing rooftops, fire dripping from the eaves like very heavy rainwater.

Blazing tongues blossomed from the upper stories of the Spa. Inside were the Carnarellis. *Oink, oink, oink!* Their cries of alarm. Frantically mother and father waddled from window to window but they were too fat to squeeze out. At their prayers were the twins, kneeling by the bedside and stark. Four identical tits plopped on the floor. As the girls sobbed and prayed for the Almighty to save them. I'll give you fifty cents, one said. I'll give you some poontang, said the other. But He was not in a saving mood today. Another bomb fell and turned the Carnarelli family into roast pork.

All over Hollinsford toilets crashed from one burning floor down to the next. On one of which sat Reverend, the shithead. He died. So did Raymond Perkins and his dad Ralph the selectman and the Orems and the Hatches and old Miss Searton the schoolteacher and the Dimicks and Dynamite Boggert who'd been to the Yukon. The kids sang: Fire, fire, go away, come again some other day. And their singing only seemed to make it worse. The roof caved in on the Cartier Club and Canucks sat there with beer in their hands and tried to get in one last gulp before Eternal Rewards were passed around. Houses toppled and ladders of sparks fluttered up in the sky. Folks lying in the street like they were sunburned, ruddy pink or scarlet.

And out came the rats. So many in such a small town. Thousands of them came, seething from the doors and windows and crevices of buildings. Or what was left of buildings. Flaming little rodents. Something in their rat fur seemed to be fine tinder. Those not already ablaze ignited like flares as they scrambled out of the burning debris. Hopped piles of crispy folks and fallen eagle emblems. And dashed in one continuous spate for the river. Poor bastards! If they thought the river would save them, they were dead wrong. They drowned. In this mission the good suffered with the bad.

By now the Chinook had dropped enough bombs to feed a nation of fire-eaters, but it returned to dump one final load on the Boone household. The old man got it first. He never knew what hit him. He scratched his little monkey head and thought it might be termites or the house settling once more. But Jeff knew. Plenty of napalm where he'd been. Help, Jesse! he hollered. The Hero could only shake his head. He was doing his duty as it was. Kindly, Jesse! his brother yelled again. But it was too late for kindly.

And Jeff's room grew brighter and brighter till, like a miniature sun, it was impossible to gaze directly at it. Jeff stood framed at the window, his clothes a cloak of fire, his hair ablaze. He jumped. Too late again! Charcoal-broiled brother. Fervid rats scampered over his carcass, cars drove back and forth over it trying to escape from town. Then with a shudder the old house itself—the old crawling house of Jesse's boyhood—collapsed into a pile of fiery planks and crossbeams. Seconds later nothing remained of it but the icebox and the TV.

That's just an awful game, Jesse. . . .

. . . and the big chopper, its job done, withdrew slowly from the scene of carnage and went back beyond the mountains. A halo of fire ringed the black and steaming ground. No Hollinsford at all. It was as though the town never existed. Some would call it sad for a town to be burned right off the face of the map. Not Jesse. He was only a bit weary from all that excitement. He backed off from the girl and zipped up his jeans. The skies were silent.

They set out again. Jesse was in a very agreeable mood. He sang of grimy gopher guts and maple syrup. Grace didn't join him this time. She couldn't sing with that glower anyway. Silent and pouty-mouthed she was a Miss Grump now. Miss Grump! Miss Grump! the boy yelled at her. Ain't no fun when you're a sourpuss, he said. His words fell on deaf ears. She walked like each step was a real effort. He moved closer to her and as he did she walked farther away. Like he harbored a bad smell. Disneyland! he declared, trying to get a reaction out of her. He did— she stuck her tongue out at him.

A pissy girl could be a real pain in the A-hole. The boy raised his hand like he was going to hit her again. It was a bluff to get her back in line. He would never hit her so soon after the last hit. He knew she'd quickly grow immune to his blows or bored with them if he hit her too often. Space them out, one or two a day and no more. That was common sense.

But the girl took off like a rabbit. Dropping her suitcase, she lit out on one of the snowmachine tracks.

Jesse was caught flatfooted. He'd expected her to say *Don't hit me please!* or *That's rough stuff!* For which he'd prepared a little speech about grumpiness. He hadn't expected her to run away like this. For a min-ute he could only stand there and watch her. And with dropped jaw wonder what made her do it. He called out to the girl: Come on back, you little bitch.

He wobbled after Grace swearing at her crazi-ness. A strange herkyjerk kind of creature, laden with a suitcase and a .22 rifle and *Motherfucker!* on his lips. He slipped along the hard snow like a novice skier. Or the Old Man of the Mountains somehow turned young.

The track the girl took followed the upper slope. It seemed to be created by someone who liked to swivel his machine around rocky outcroppings. It

wound west through a pine grove and a patch of
hemlocks and at one point Jesse was able to see the
dump with all its trash sparkling in the sun. At
another point he could see the town of Northton
sprawled between two distant ridges. He tried to pick
out the Miracle Mile but he tripped over some stone
or submerged root and fell—he should have known
not to run in one direction and stare in another. And
his gun went flying into a snowbank. He was all right
but he wondered about the rimfire. He took it up gently, dusted off the snow and apologized to it. It's that
Grace's fault, he said.

The track switchbacked and Jesse found himself
in familiar territory, the tower and the girl's suitcase
ahead of him and the girl herself just ahead of that.
Geez but she's going in circles, he thought.

Soon the track divided into two and the girl was
swaying toward the back haunch of the hill. Jesse pur-
sued her as best he could, considering the weight of
all his weapons. But the gap was widening between
them. Slow girl, hah! That showed how much Jeff
knew. Far from being slow, the girl seemed like she
was powered by a V-8 engine. And now she was only
a green-coated speck.

The boy hollered: I'll rip your guts out if you
don't come back. Right away he wished he hadn't said
anything for what girl in her right mind would run
back to have her guts ripped out? Won't rip them out,
he shouted, correcting himself. But it didn't make a
bit of difference. No more effect on her than ripping
her guts out. She still ran.

And he passed the tower and an overturned garbage bin and he passed the stone cairn dedicated to
the Indian chief who jumped. Before long he was on
the back slope and looking toward the huge white

hump of rock that was Mount Washington. Where
the sun was no more. That same sun lay behind the
boy now, in what he guessed was the direction of
Vermont. Where the hell was Vietnam supposed to
be? It seemed to flop around like a fish out of water.
But unlike a fish he couldn't whop its head and
thereby kill it. He had to find it, not kill it, and that
might be easier said than done in this white New
Hampshire wilderness.

Worried boy. Fretfurrowed brow. He was moving into the teeth of an east wind now and it slammed
at his neck and face and sent needlelike prickles
roaming beneath his winter coat. They felt like stings
from a thousand smutty bees. He turned his face this
way and that but the wind couldn't seem to get
enough of him. Scram! he yelled at it. The wind didn't
scram.

Soldier without a war. He almost wished he was
back home watching the war rather than searching for
it. His happy eyes but a foot or two from a commando
raid. *Give 'em hell, fellows! Tear those yellow skins off their
backs! Attaway!* Bentnecked little bad guy bodies in a
wallow of mud. His old man would arrive with a fold-
up table and a plate of his all-time favorites. Supper,
boy. And eating his fill or more than his fill Jesse
would think himself the luckiest boy in the whole
wide world. He'd belch his appreciation to his father.

And now he came to a place where the hill
dipped sharply. The track was washed over by little
rivulets of melting snow and polished to a slickness.
Jesse was so glad to escape that frightful wind that he
forgot to slow down. His feet were turning on the ice
like wheels. They went one way and he went the
other, plummeting down headfirst, doused in the
snow, the goddamned snow again. He went through

the hardedged crust and into a bed of softer snow which closed around him. In his rage he bashed at it with his fists, then with his head. Stupid girl.

The boy got up and felt around and dug out his rifle. Then he saw Grace sitting on a flat rock not a hundred feet below him. Worn out from her stunt. Stay there or I'll shoot! he shouted. She jumped up and began scurrying down the path again. Jesse in his hunter's pose, raising the rimfire to shoulder level. He'd fire a shot or two to put the fear of God in her.

Sighting above Grace's head Jesse pulled back the trigger. Nothing happened, not even a click. He knocked out the impacted snow from when he'd used the rifle as a walking stick and tried again, with the same result. He looked down the barrel to see could he discover what ailed the gun. He shook it and put his ear to the place above the trigger where he reckoned the heart to be. He believed the gun might be dead. No one ever told him about the bolt action.

Meanwhile the girl was again putting tracks between them. She disappeared around a bend. Jesse toyed with the gun a while longer and then with a certain reluctance gave up the idea of shooting at his girl. He gave up on the gun, too. It was one piece of metal that didn't last. He flung it off in disgust. Fortunately he still had his tommy. And certain potent items of kitchenware.

It was a downhill that at least gave his body some peace. The track puppeted him down with hardly any effort on his part. Somewhere below he heard a stream rush along the hillside with water from the dying winter. It had a muted internal sound, like intestinal rumblings inside the earth itself. And the boy imagined his Grace carelessly stumbling into that stream, perhaps smashing her thin little skull so hard on a hidden rock that her palate dropped into her mouth, perhaps getting dragged down to some underground lake filled with huge girl-eating monsters, or just knocked unconscious, that would do the trick, and the water flooding into her mouth till she drowned. He shivered at the prospect of his girl coming to such a bad end. For he still loved her though she was a bitch.

Toward the bottom he was slogging through a morass of snow and slush. His feet were cold, he was miserable. He told the wet gray ground to go to hell.

Jesse heard a snowmachine skir through the woods, its sound magnified many times by the hilly spaces. A gray jay flew over him, dipped down to take a closer look and as though he was of little consequence it whisked quickly away to a distant treetop and screeched like a hawk, *teacup, teacup.* The hill was done with pulling the boy now. It leveled off to a straightaway, and the track passed through a spruce marsh and went into a stretch of boulders that looked like a sea suddenly turned to stone, still boasting its crests and hollows and overhanging waves, and pierced with hundreds of little potholes. Jesse guessed they'd grown up in this place from small pebbles and in time they'd grow even more, pushing aside trees and mounds of earth, huge bodiless heads of stone.

One of these boulders was crying ever so softly, sniffing and sobbing like a little girl. Unhappy stony thing. Jesse in search of that sobbing. At the end of the chase, a bucket of tears. He didn't have far to look. His girl hadn't even bothered to hide. At a junction of trails she lay in full view, her lean body twisted against a boulder, her face buried in the curve of her arm, in rock. Blubbering for Lord knows what reason. Perhaps she wanted her mommy, perhaps even her daddy now. Small afflicted gasps from the depths.

Jesse's first thought was to hit her. Hitting was one of only a very few things a person could do to a girl. It was what he'd wanted to do to her all during that long and tiresome chase. He kicked her lightly on the leg and she turned an unsurprised face toward him and he raised his hand like it was a tomahawk. Give her a good scalping for all the trouble she'd caused. Time to take your medicine, he said. Her big sorrowful eyes said there'd been already too much medicine as it was. Wet snotnosed girl. Red hair twined with a crust of snow and ice, clothes splotched—she looked like some huge stump of a foot had ground her through the snow into the earth below. Jesse couldn't seem to force his hand down into that eggshell face. Nor could he even knot his hand into a fist now. He dropped down beside the trembling girl and all of a sudden he started to cry himself, who would have believed it, Hero Jesse turning on the Niagara. Wild racking sobs. Onto Grace's breast and into her hair he poured all the tears dammed up since he'd left home and maybe even before that. They came in such earthquakey shudders, they might have been there since he was born. He cried because he was tired and hungry and his feet hurt and he needed a nap, and he cried because he'd never find the snow-machine track to Vietnam, never in a million years of footslogging it through these harsh hills. No friend now, that great out-of-doors, but just a place he'd never been before and he'd always been struck dumb and helpless when lost in a land that wasn't Hollinsford. Crying like a baby he was a baby now. And through his baby tears or as a result of them he saw himself stark and crawling on his hands and knees down cold tracks, no more notion of how to get to Vietnam than he had of tying his shoelaces in the morning. The action was wherever he wasn't. To shadow it forever was his fate. That's what recon meant—no action. Buckets of tears for life. With all his heart the boy wished for a crib or a TV or anything like a box that would bury him inside its four warm walls. Poor little retard come and rest your head on your old dad's arm. I'm scared, dad. No reason to be scared, it's only a dream. You go back to sleep now. For you're dad's boy and dad loves you very much.

But there was no dad in the whole wide world. And so the boy put both his arms around Grace and their salt tears mixed together like droplets of a lost spindrift from the faraway faraway sea.

PART V
Lost and Found

It was coming on dusk when the snowmachine raced past them, backed up, and jolted to a stop in front of them. Cuddled in each other's arms they were struggling to keep warm. Weary children. Sad whining puppy noises from the rocks. They didn't see the man standing over them. They could not have said how long he stood there. You runaways? he asked at last.

Jesse looked up. Phillip Holderness. In his hand a thirty-thirty Winchester. His left eyelid half-shut and something like a blackberry mired inside. Nose squashed from where a tree had fallen on it. Brute logger. The boy's old man had warned him time and again to stay away from the Holderness brothers.

You runaways? the man repeated.

Jesse climbed to his feet. You know how to get to Vietnam from here? he asked in an anxious voice.

Right away the man grinned. Vietnam? Don't rightfully know. I'm 4-F myself, he said, pointing to his buckshot eye.

Well, I'm fixing to go there. . . .

I bet you are, pal. The logger turned to Grace: You going to Vietnam too, honey?

Slowly the girl pulled down the bars of her fingers from her face and gazed up at the man. She shook her head in such a way that it was not possible to tell whether she meant yes or no. Jesse answered for her: She's going for the sunshine. . . .

She's a piece of sunshine herself. You're Sam

151

Pettigrew's girl Grace, aren't you? Your daddy know you're up here with this young devil, Grace? A little jump'n squirt in the snow, eh Grace? A little in-and-out-and-wipe-it? The man's grin now seemed to take up his whole head. As he talked his rifle swayed from side to side. The barrel caught little glints of light and Jesse couldn't help but gape at it. Back and forth, back and forth. Drawn as to a hypnotist's watch.

Can I hold your gun? the boy pleaded. Can I kindly hold it for a second?

You know, a fellow gets pretty lonely holed up in these woods. Nothing but trees as company. My brother Andy's gone away. . . .

. . . kilt Hack, didn't he?

. . . and so I'm all by my lonesome. Tell you what. You don't want to be sitting outdoors on a cold night like tonight. Christ knows what'll be prowling around here. Wolves. Maybe even a few panthers. Why don't you come back with me to my camp? Me and Andy, we done up the old Bryson sugaring-off shack. Cozy as can be. We'll have a big cheery fire and roast some marshmallows. How's that sound? He was staring at Grace, his lone eye aimed at her shaking body. Then he glanced at the boy: And pal, I'll let you hold my gun all you want. Maybe even let you take it out back and do some plinking with it.

What about Vietnam? Jesse asked.

Hell, Vietnam's a whole other ball game. You're smart enough, you oughter know you can't go there this time a day. Best get an early start in the morning. And Phillip Holderness motioned them over to his machine. Jesse gasped at what he saw there. Swathed in burlap on the cushion was a set of huge hindquarters. Thought the boy: Water buffalo! He asked Phillip if he'd been out hunting.

No sir. That's just a big hunk of raw beefsteak for our dinner. Tenderloin on the haunch. Finest cut there is. You like beefsteak?

Eyes dancing, Jesse admitted that he did. He said he preferred it to water buffalo steak. And if he needed any more convincing, here it was—good steak dinner in his gut, a night's rest, and he'd be fit as a fiddle to hit the road tomorrow. He might even ask Phillip Holderness for a map.

The man told Grace to hop aboard and put her arms around his waist. Only for support, he tittered. And he directed the boy to sit atop the load of beefsteak in the rear. Shove his legs under the twine that held it down.

But I can't reach you from back here. . . .

You hold on to your girl, loony!

And they tore off into the woods. An up-country track. The snowmachine swiveled around banks and corners like a toboggan. Its light turned birch trees into ghosts standing by the wayside. Jesse lost his lumberjack's cap. He yelled to stop but his voice was swept up by the roar of the motor.

They crossed a tote road and another tote road and turned down a go-back and at last they arrived at the shack. One big eye of a window greeted them with a mirror of the snowmachine's own lights. For an instant the shack burst into a dim glowing life. Pointed tarpapery roof. Ovenpipe chimney. Overhang for the skidder. They went in and were greeted by spokes of cold air. Dull thuds were their steps, not creaks or cannons. Phillip lit a kerosene lamp. And the boy, who expected to see a big vat and syrup tins, saw only two cots and a table and woodstove, bare ground for a floor and brush scattered around it. A girlie calendar hung on the wall.

Grace blurted out: It's just like where Our Lord was born. . . .

Sure is, honey, Phillip declared as he went over to the stove.

At Sunday school they said it was a place like this, the girl went on. A little tiny barn, no floor, hay all over . . .

. . . that's just brush for his fire, I bet, Jesse said.

Only it had a lot of animals. Cows and cats, dogs. You got any animals here?

Only her, Phillip said, pointing to the naked girl on the calendar.

Our Lord wasn't born here, was He? Jesse asked the man.

Piling logs into the stove Phillip said something about he wasn't so sure. Girl had brains. She might know a damn sight more about it than us men. He lit some newspaper and tossed it in the stove and with a *whoosh!* a fire was raging there. Stove's faster on the draw than John Wayne, he said.

A quietly superior look on Grace's face. See, she said. Place just like this.

This place's for sugaring-off, Jesse said.

You don't know because you don't go to Sunday school. . . .

Said Jesse: Us men got brains, too. . . . He was willing to concede that she might know a little more about births or whatever and the stables where they sometimes took place. In fact, births might be her specialty. But how many folks had she killed? How many Hacks knocked off? Gooks bayonetted? How many witches had she clobbered in her time? That, to the boy, was the crux of the matter.

If you got brains then why don't you help me with them hindquarters? said Phillip. Jesse eagerly ran outside ahead of him. Man's work. Girls had their births and men hauled ass, worked their fingers to the bone. He grappled with the twine that held down the massive haunch, tugging at it with all his might. Grind. He seized a flap of meat and was heave-hoing with it when Phillip came out. Shit fella you'll rupture yourself blue. I only asked you out here for a little talk. He put his arm on the boy's shoulder. Man-to-man talk. He told Jesse: Can really use me a little piece tonight. Fella gets sick and tired of those Canuck whores that can swallow up a stud horse. The boy looked at him. He didn't know about Canuck whores but he was so hungry he could eat a horse himself. Phillip said: Know what I mean? The boy licked his chops. Glad you do because after supper I'd like you to take a little walk. . . .

And Jesse said: Take a little walk? Where? Look for Hack some more?

You know. Disappear for a while.

The boy didn't know. Was it for the exercise or what? But he didn't want the man to think him a dummy so he said yes, he'd disappear. Be a ghost.

Phillip smiled and told him that he was a true buddy. Anytime the boy needed a saddle of venison, just give a hoot. And then he climbed into his machine and drove it backwards to the shack and straight through the door. Grace jumped up, cupped her hands to her ears. With three or four swipes of his knife the man had the twine cut and the haunch dropped to the floor. No need to be afraid, honey, he said to the girl, it's just meat. . . .

Beefsteak, Jesse added.

The man cut through the bone with a handsaw. He drew his sheath knife upwards using a clean hilt-to-point stroke. Jesse moved in for a closer inspection.

Magic to him how an animal was turned into food.
Did that animal in its animal head know it was food?
The boy thought it'd be nice to know. A shame this
cow's head wasn't around so that he could look into
the matter. Pry into the brain for its secrets.

Phillip was now trimming off the fat. Jesse
moved closer yet. How he wished his old man could
have gone out and killed a cow and brought its
haunch home some night for supper!

Watch it, pal, said the man, or you'll end up like
Bob Siddall. . . .

. . . no nose . . .

You get the picture.

No words to describe it.

Sure ain't. Hole in the middle of your face. Back
off.

On the stove sat a skillet gray inside with an inch
of grease. Phillip raised it like an axe and crashed it
down on the floor and cold globs spattered onto
Grace's coat. The girl had her hands over her eyes
now. She didn't seem to care for all that lovely red
meat. But Jesse cared enough for both of them. He
couldn't wait to sink his chops into it. His eyes attended the swaths of the man's knife. Thick steaks
were carved off the porous ham and shoulder bones.
The boy's head took up the same motion. Froth came
to his mouth. All he needed now was his old friend
the TV. He asked Phillip where he kept his. The man
shook his head. No electricity, he said.

Don't wanna see 'lectricity. I wanna see TV,
wanna see TV, wanna see TV . . .

Phillip glanced up from his knife work and spat.
He said: You got eyes in your head, boy? Can't you
see we don't got . . . hey you throwing a fit or something. . . .

Already Jesse had switched on the TV that he carried around with him for emergencies like this one. Newstime, boy. Come and get it. War's on. Bright snowless screen with that turkey Shanahan shambling out of the jungle. Shanahan ordered him to dig those latrines but fast. The platoon would soon be back. After a day of destroy missions, they'd want the peace and quiet of a good shit. Replied Hero Jesse: I'm a soldier not a shithouse man. Send you back to New Hampshire, Shanahan threatened. And the Hero made a face at the very thought of returning to New Hampshire. Folks back there would call him pansyassed. They'd giggle at him in the street. Kids would make up rhymes about coward Jesse. With Grace at his side he'd come too far, stormed the white altitudes of too many mountains, to go back now. And so he threatened Shanahan right back: Send you home to Ohio . . . At that the gobbler reached for his gun. Jesse was quicker. He unsheathed his hunting knife and jabbed it into the fat of the man's chest and jabbed it again. He slit Shanahan open and hauled forth the steaming guts (Gimme back my guts! Shanahan squealed), never seen so few guts in a man before, three or four at most, the yellowbellied bastard. He slashed off the man's cobra tattoo and cut it into dozens of little cobras and scattered them to the four winds. For good measure he cut off Shanahan's nose. And by the time he got through the turkey looked like he'd been dressed for Thanksgiving dinner. The grunts gathered around and gawked at their dead CO. One of them turned to the Hero: I guess you're our new leader now, huh? And Jesse merely nodded, he being the strong silent type who spoke with his weapons, like, for instance, this knife.

. . . or you just copying me? grinned Phillip.

They sat down to a late supper. Tenderloin fillets garnished with onions and butter. Sizzling in tin mess plates. Now don't tell me that isn't fit for a king, the logger said.

King or not, it wasn't fit for Grace. She didn't seem to care for the meat cooked any more than she liked the looks of it raw. Leaning down nearly to her plate she'd munch at a piece of meat and then take that piece all raggedy and half-chewed from her mouth and deposit it in her coat pocket. Good manners, thought Jesse. A guest in the man's house but she won't say she doesn't like the grub. As for himself, he was never hungrier. He could have eaten a plate of dogspew if one was set before him. The whole day he'd had only a single doughnut and a tin of bologna. Meager fare for a growing boy. He harnessed every last bit of his energy in getting that meat to his mouth and down his throat to the empty space that was his tummy. His teeth knew no rest. From time to time he removed the little half-chewed wads of meat from Grace's pocket and ate them. Phillip gazed at them both as though they were visitors from Mars.

Fit for a king, Jesse said, making his animal noises.

The logger chuckled. You ever eat a moose before?

Thud! Something landed on the roof. The scrape of claws along tarpaper. A deep rasping whinnying sound. Phillip jumped up. Camp thief! he exclaimed. And he grabbed his rifle and headed out the door. Grace asked the boy what a camp thief was. The only thing he could think of was a Canuck. Moments later they heard a gunshot and the soft thump-thump of some creature's body (too small for a Canuck, Jesse felt) rolling down the roof grade. Phillip returned to the shack holding a raccoon. Dead bandit face. Dead yellowish underfur. A trickle of blood issued from the peppery flank. Grace screamed as though in pain. The logger flung the animal by the tail into the corner, where it lay like a crumpled rug. Breakfast, he said.

Coon porridge, agreed Jesse.

Grace's face held a silent mask of suffering which quickly became tears. Oh poor little thing, she sobbed. Poor poor little thing . . .

Jee-sus! snorted Jesse.

. . . little raccoon didn't hurt no one . . .

Aw c'mon Grace, don't. . . . From the way she was crying, a person would think she'd lost her loving family in a car wreck.

Got a nest of babies back home, I bet. . . .

Not likely, Phillip said. This here's a boy raccoon. This time a year they wander from den to den looking for girl raccoons. Call it raccoontang, heh, heh . . . And with his one eye the man gave a wink to Jesse, who winked back at him even though he didn't much care for girl raccoons (give him girls instead) himself. But Phillip must like them. The Canucks had their rats, let the logger screw coons. The boy was tolerant of such things. He was less tolerant of all those fruitcake tears. He wished Grace would stop crying. It embarrassed him around other people. Us men don't like crybabies, he told the girl. You quit or I'll tell you a bad thing about your daddy. . . .

The girl turned on Jesse. Temper breaking through her tears. And you wanted me to help kill you some gophers! I'll never do it! Never!

It wasn't gophers, you dope. . . .

Now, now, the logger said. She ain't no more a dope than you are. . . . And he touched the girl's hair,

her cheeks. He moved his hand along her leg, back
and forth in strokes that ranged wide.

That's her pussy, Jesse explained.

I wanna go home now, the girl cried.

Can't. Your daddy's eaten by rats. . . .

His words did not cause her tears to abate.
C'mon, the logger told him, let's you and me have
ourselves a beer. Don't know why, but a woman crying always makes me want a beer.

Always makes me want a milk, the boy said.

Got no milk. It's beer or skillet grease. . . . He
placed a six-pack on the table. For good reason Jesse
looked at that six-pack hesitantly. Etched in his mind
were certain images of drink and doom. Pierre the
Pisser all geezed up and carving away like mad at his
wife. Officer Granville's head rolling merrily down
Route 123 (according to Reverend, that's what happened to people drunk on duty). Louis Lamarre
downing a quart of kerosene from Thibodeaux's Market. Found the next day with his hand down his throat
like he wanted to pull something out. Then there was
Jim Carney, who mistook Wendum's Pond for his
bathtub and drowned as he tried to scrub his back.
And Hack. A person couldn't very well forget him.
Drink led to the trucker's downfall, too.

Can't you flip it open by yourself? Phillip said.
And he flipped open the top of one of the beer cans
for the boy. He nudged it across to him. Some beer
spilled out, a trail of snail slime along the birch table.
The boy tasted it with his finger. It tasted a little like
snail slime, too. Man's drink. And it dawned on him
that he was a man. Hell, one beer wouldn't wreck his
brains. Or kill him as the others had been killed. Of
that he could be sure, for the Almighty would inter-
cede for him at the first sign of trouble. No volleyball
of a head on Route 123 for Hero Jesse.

The boy swallowed. He tried not to make a face. Stinging nettles all the way down to his toes, all the way up again. He dared not spit them out. Instead he pulled out his deepest voice. Been logging any lately? he asked Phillip. He was hoping for another one of those man-to-man talks.

Can't. They got my brother locked up. . . .

Your brother kill Hack?

The logger laughed. He hawked up a gob. A yellow quarter stained the floor. Wish he'd killed someone, he said. At least then there'd be a good reason. Not just some damage to some old property over in Bethel . . .

Plowed his jeep into the church . . .

Yeah. Hey, how'd you know?

Friends with the cops, Jesse confessed. He took a big sip from his beer to prove it.

You don't say. . . . The man lit a cigarette. Well, you tell your friends the cops . . .

. . . machinegunned our outhouse . . . my orders . . .

You tell them I can't do no work around here without my brother. Logging's a two-man job. One man by himself's hardly any good. . . .

Takes teamwork . . .

Right. Need someone to tell you which way your tree's gonna fall. Best to keep it in the family. Best mate's your brother. Some old froggy ain't gonna give a good goddamn if a birch tree cuts you in two. Nah, he'll pray to Holy Jesus for it to happen. One less of us means one more froggy coming down here to work.

I know, Jesse said. Hell, don't I know that. . . .

Then you tell your cops to let Andy out on probation or something. I miss the old dough-re-mi. Tell them they're taking cash out of my pocket. . . .

Like Andy done to Hack . . .

I wish you'd stop saying that. You're talking about my brother. . . .

Another swig from the can for grown-up Jesse. One brother by himself's hardly any good, he said.

That's true. That's what I been telling you. . . .

Everything's best when it's brothers. Brothers rule the roost. Fight gooks. Can't cut them apart with any ol' hunting knife. Glue's too strong.

The beer was going to the boy's head. Jesse aswim in a strange yellow sea. Rough waters. Small craft. Someone else took over the controls and said, Kill for a brother. . . .

Yeah. Forgot about that. You got a brother, too.

Baby brother. I watch over him.

Wait. I thought you was the younger one. . . .

I'm the Vietnam one. Bravo Company. That's the one I am.

Phillip appeared to understand now. Sure you are, he said, laughing. Bet they put you in charge of Army Intelligence, too. . . .

Brother stays home. Can't hardly dress himself in the morning or tie his own shoelaces. But I'm proud of that boy all the same.

Of course. Nothing like having a retard in the family.

Nothing like it . . .

The logger crushed his empty beer can and settled back in his chair and regarded the boy with some amusement, as though he'd never set sight on anything like him before. Every now and then he glanced over at Grace. The girl was no longer crying. Instead she was putting chunks of leftover meat into her hair, tying them into neat little knots. They dangled there like baubles on some kind of savage. Don't you want to look pretty for me, Grace? Phillip asked her. And she smiled. She *was* looking pretty for him.

Could use me another beer, Jesse said.

You'll be a logger yet, pal. . . . And as the man flipped open another beer there came from the roof a sound like a falling body. Camp thief! the boy shouted. Grace immediately put her head in Phillip's lap and said in a soft stricken voice, Oh please don't kill this one please mister kindly. . . . Phillip began to pet her and at the same time he tried to remove some of the meat she'd tied to her hair. Now don't you worry, he said. It isn't no coon this time. Only a little snow melting off the roof. It must be getting warmer out there. Springtime coming, and you know what they say about springtime, don't you, Grace?

The girl shook her head.

They say springtime's for lovers. . . .

They wanted to send my brother to Concord, Jesse said. But I wouldn't let 'em. Love that boy. Wouldn't want him cooped up. . . .

But the logger was still attending to Grace. You look warm, honey. . . . He helped the girl off with her coat. There now, don't you feel more comfortable? By way of an answer she asked him if he had any animals in his manger. Maybe little puppies? Live little puppies?

Jesse: I watch over my brother and the Almighty watches over me.

You'd be surprised what watches over us, pal, the man said. Some day I expect the curtains to open up on the sky . . .

Our Lord?

. . . and some big old whore to shout, I fucked you all, every last one of you, and what's more I gave you all the clap.

Some big old horsie, Grace repeated after him.
You got one here?

No but I got a little stallion that'll do you just
fine. And turning to Jesse the logger said: Remember
that walk I mentioned a while back? I think it's time
you took it. . . .

And the boy tried how he tried to take his walk.
For he promised the man and he wanted to be as good
as his word. He stood woozily and staggered around
the shack hunting high and low for the door. He
couldn't seem to find it. Stupid door up and walked
away on him. He had no way out now. Finally his
oceantossed body found a mooring at one of the cots.
He lifted his feet and stretched out his legs and puked
up Jonah again and again. Far more came out than
he'd ever put in. Half his innards were spreading in a
dull thick puddle on the cot. And in his own sickness
he lay his head and whether he was asleep or awake
retching he could not have said. He did, however, see
his baby brother sinking slowly through the green
depths to the bottom of the sea.

Don't mister. . . .

Grace's words sounded like they were miles
away and spoken through gauze. The boy turned his
head. A lead weight of a head. And he watched from
what seemed like the next county as the girl's dress—
gauze as well—was swept from her body. Hands rac-
ing like huge excited moths over her thin chest and
thighs. Logger at work. Her slip and undies plopped
to the floor.

Don't like this game at all. . . .

All Jesse could see now was the man's buckrab-
biting rear end. His girl buried under Phillip Holderness. It occurred to him that the logger was assaulting
her. Assault. The word leaped to him out of nowhere.

Lay on his tongue like it would burn a hole there. He called out for the man to stop. He said Grace was his girl. Phillip told him to fuck off pal.

At that the boy stumbled over to the other cot and pounded on the man's back. *You pervert!* The logger pushed him away and he fell facedown on the floor. Mouthful of dirt. Stars in his eyes. He charged back and tried to shake the logger loose from his girl. Phillip was stuck fast. *You stop that! You oughter be ashamed of yourself!* The man laughed and flailed out with his boot and struck Jesse a solid blow in the stomach. This blow didn't hurt so much as it just made him want to puke up Jonah all over again. The boy went over to the stove and unloaded into an empty stewpot. Even now not wanting to leave a mess. Even now mindful of good manners.

Lie still you little bitch! gasped the logger.

And then the boy was done with being sick. Bravo Company took over from him. Phillip Holderness would dearly pay for his fun. Assaulting someone else's girl. Jesse went for Phillip's Winchester. Hardly bothering to aim he pulled back on the trigger. The loud crack jolted the rafters. From Phillip's back spurted blood all bright and red. The man shrieked but still seemed to wriggle as before. Jesse fired again. To get the man off his Grace once and for all. This time he hit him in the arm. The logger craned his head to see what was shooting at him. His mouth gaped open like he was about to say something. And the boy told him he was a sonofabitch and a pervert and fired a third time and got him in the neck. Phillip's body jerked to a standstill.

It was nice to fire a semi-automatic for a change. The boy looked down at a job well done. The deadest logger he'd ever seen. The man's cock was still rigid.

See what happens? Jesse said to it. He shoved the man away hoping his girl would jump up and thank him with a kiss. But Grace stayed put. She looked like someone had taken a paintbrush and painted her naked body red. Holderness blood. He guessed the Holdernesses, like the Staleys, were bleeders.

The girl's deereyes stared fixedly up at the roof beams. Jesse raised his own eyes to see what she was staring at. Grace, you awake? he asked. He shook her. Skin slippery from all that blood. Her hands clenched the blanket tightly. Wisps of blanket caught in her nails. Like her fingers were in flower.

C'mon Grace don't you play dead with me. . . .

But she didn't seem to be playing at all. Or even alive. She didn't have any breath or (Jesse put his ear to her bloodsoaked chest) heartbeat. The two danger signs of death. He shook her again. How could she be dead? He'd shot Phillip Holderness, not her. He wouldn't shoot his girl for anything. But then he saw a surge of blood issuing from the upper part of her chest. More blood came from the area just below her ribs. And the boy knew he'd been a dummy, a real dummy, not to remember that when a bullet went in, it often came out again and went into something else. In this case, Grace. The same bullets that killed Phillip had killed her. And with this realization he gave the logger's body a fierce kick. Wicked person. He bashed at the man's head as he'd kick a football. He intended to kick it until it came off. But Jonah cried up to him, demanding to be let out again. He went back to his stewpot. Dry heaves and tears mingled. Spasms seized his tummy and would not release it and twisted the rest of his body taut in a series of nasty jerks. Another minute and he thought his very bones would come up next. Then suddenly Jonah was satisfied. The spasms subsided and the boy's breath stretched itself out into a long bubbly sigh. He returned to life but he nearly wished he hadn't, for he was now without Grace.

Tearfully Jesse knelt down beside the cot and prayed to the Almighty kindly to bring back his girl. He said: She didn't do You no harm she was just Grace. . . . He prayed and waited for he knew not how long. The kerosene lamp flickered and went out. The boy was left kneeling in the dark.

Gray dawn, and raw. Cloudwrapped sky. Flurries. And Jesse emerging from the sugarhouse with Grace's body, dragging it behind him like an oversized ragdoll. Hand clasped to hand—whose was colder would be hard to say.

He couldn't leave his girl to lie cold and rotting next to Phillip Holderness. Sharing her death with the person largely to blame for it. If all-the-way dead she was. Jesse wasn't so sure. He still knew so little about death and its disguises. The new day filled him with hope. He reckoned the Almighty could easily have a change of heart and bring the girl back to life. Maybe He'd been out on call last night and not even heard the boy's prayers. Jesse vowed to offer up new prayers at the first bed he came to. He'd promise to be an even better boy than he'd already been—in return for Grace.

And he couldn't very well leave the girl behind with Vietnam ahead of them. That warm corn weather might just thaw her out.

Despite everything, he didn't feel too bad. He even sought to whistle. Dusting off Phillip improved his outlook on this his world. It reminded him of his bright future. The great out-of-doors, only yesterday his enemy, could do as it damn well pleased now. It could huff and puff and drop avalanches on him. Wind giants could crack their whips against his face. Or it could turn pansy and flick flurries at him as it was doing this moment. But what it couldn't do was reel off a few rounds on a Winchester. That honor was reserved for Hero Jesse.

The girl seemed as light as goosedown, though she'd gotten a little stiff during the night. He brought her around to the back of the shack and stood her against the outhouse while he took a leak inside. She had already taken her leak. Then he took her back in front and they followed the skidder track into a birch wood. Before long they hit a tote road that appeared to head towards the south.

Now he dragged the girl, now hauled her over his shoulder. His head was throbbing like dozens of tiny blacksmiths with their hammers had invaded it. His first hangover ever. It could have been worse. That head dribbling down the highway like Officer Granville's. Lucky boy. Hardly the worse for wear. His own head might hurt a little but his head hardly mattered anyway. More important were his legs and they seemed to be as sturdy as ever. Right now he was walking as fast as he usually walked when there was no one flung over his shoulder.

Sang the road: Left, right, left, right, Hero had one helluva night. . . .

They moved past a yard of downed timber waiting to be toted. Birch logs stacked up in neat piles. The boy guessed they were some of Phillip's work. Trees dead as the man who cut them. He stopped and blew a raspberry at them.

The track joined a wider track which bore signs of recent travel. Snowmachines. The heavy tread of a

pulp truck. Jesse walked more slowly now. He didn't
want to be seen with Grace as long as she was in this
condition. Folks would not understand.

Up ahead he heard the scrape and buzz of a chain
saw. In a clearing he saw the figure of a man working
the limbs off a fallen tree. He dropped Grace into a
snowdrift. She sank down with only her face showing
and he soon had that covered up. If anyone happened
along now, they'd think the girl was just more snow.

Jesse approached the man whom he recognized
as Denis Lamarre, Canuck. Hi, he said. His voice
couldn't be heard above the saw so he tapped the man
on the back. Denis Lamarre all but cut his arm off in
surprise. He shut off the saw and gave the boy a surly
look.

You got a map? Jesse asked. He figured he could
read a map simply by staring at it.

Denis Lamarre's mouth worked around a plug of
tobacco. Hey ain't you that guy they been looking
for?

Nah. That's my brother.

Hell but ain't you Jesse Boone. . . .

Never was, never will be. I only want a map.

The man's eyes narrowed. He pointed his finger.
You're that runaway. . . .

The boy said: Well, have fun with your trees. . . .
And trying to whistle he headed back towards the
road. He could feel those little frog eyes burrowing
into his back. A person couldn't even trust a Canuck
for a map anymore. They had to get your whole life
story first. They, of all people, who dealt in wife
chopping and warts and rotgut. Troublemakers.
Ralph Perkins the selectman once said: Bomb the
Hollow and you'll get rid of nearly all the crime in
this county. Jesse agreed.

He heard the chain saw start up again and he figured Denis Lamarre preferred grind to him. For the moment. No telling what the man would do if he saw the Hero with Grace. Denis looked like the type to call out the Marines. Get them runaways! Lock 'em up! Jesse did hope to meet the Marines but not as a runaway. So he didn't care to risk another run-in with Denis. He decided to put to use the detour trick he'd learned from the TV. He'd circle through the woods and come out on the other side of the road from his enemy. Folks used this trick against Indians and dinosaurs.

The boy returned to where he'd left Grace and dug her up. Fortunately he'd thought to provide her with her coat. Better that than bare skin in this weather. He whisked the snow off her hair and face, and from the coat fuzz. There now, he said, you're good as new. He grabbed her hand again and they struck out for the woods.

Yesterday's warm weather had put a hard crust on the snow and Jesse found he could walk on it though there was no track. Not so the girl. She seemed to be fair game for everything that came her way. Her coat sleeves caught on half-buried branches. Her hair was snagged on brush and bits of scrog and he had to go back and rip it loose. The fingers on her hand clutched at things. That was because they had curled up and set.

He shifted her to his shoulder again. And with the extra weight he sank through the crust and almost to his knees. He went on walking or trying to walk. The snow didn't let his legs move as they usually moved, one after the other, marching forward like clockwork. He had to lift them high in order to move at all. He was slower than cold molasses. It was boot camp all over again. The Hero, rifle in hand, stepping through a field of old rubber tires. Grind. And so he tried the other shoulder. Same result. He tried carrying the girl couched in his arms. That was no good, either. And holding her in his arms he was not able to balance himself. Two steps and he tipped over backwards and the girl's head clunked against his and as they both hit the ground she landed on top of him. Blueskinned girl. Her body felt like a piece of wooden planking.

Ain't really doing your share, are you? he told the girl, touching her face not without affection. For she was still his Grace, dead weight though she was right now. He couldn't leave her alone in the snowy woods. How would she manage without him?

By now Jesse was convinced Grace would return to her old self before very long. Scream out if he killed some little animal, if he strangled, say, a chickadee or a sparrow. The boy assumed there'd be a laying on of large hands in the next day or so. Hadn't his own cousin Ezra Steere come back from the dead the year before? Ezra had a seizure bowling candlepins and he was lost to the world for two days and then came alive and asked the doctors first thing had he bowled a strike. True, he walked with a limp after that and he could hardly remember who was in his family and who not. But then Ezra never seemed to like his family anyway. He beat the living tar out of his wife and kids. The dog, too. God was only trying to help him out by making him forget. As for the limp, that was God's way of showing He was still boss.

If the Almighty helped Ezra like that, He'd surely help Grace. The girl was special. Heavenly birth. Nothing heavenly about Ezra Steere. He smelled like his pockets were always full of ripe hog guts.

By this simple faith Jesse was governed. Not for nothing had he attended church all those years. They said he hadn't listened in church. It wasn't true. They said he only went there to giggle at Reverend or pry loose pieces of black and hardened gum from underneath the pews. They didn't realize that was his way of listening.

Once more he bent down and heaved Grace over his shoulder. The two of them were powdered with snow. He shook himself and the girl and again began those heavy tottering steps. Left . . . right . . . left . . . right . . . ain't gonna hit . . . Vietnam . . . tonight. But he didn't care. Vietnam had waited for him this long, it could wait another day or two. He grinned. He still felt good about killing Phillip. He found himself believing in a war that never ran out of gooks no matter how late a person arrived. His tardiness only meant he'd be bringing up the rear flank. The cleverest generals, he knew, were found in the rear.

A red squirrel sputtered and barked at him, its tail snapping in anger. Jesse sputtered back at it. Nuts to you, pal, he said. He moved on and crossed an old dry-stone wall marking the line of someone's farm long ago, lifetimes before his. They were lifetimes that were shaggy woods now. Folks gone to seed, pine and maple forever after. At least he didn't have to worry about that happening to him. No one would stick a tap into his trunk. Not where he was going.

By now the boy figured he'd outwitted Denis Lamarre twice and three times over. Time to head back. Shuffling Grace to his other shoulder he trudged alongside the stone wall. He thought that would take him back to the road. He thought people built their walls starting from a road. Where else would they start? In the middle of nowhere?

The woods were getting thicker. Dense evergreens rose sheeted and ghostly and cluttered the sky. Twig tips like fingers in white gloves. He came to a hummock of spruce trees. The wall ended abruptly in a scattering of stones. Those lost-looking stones did not fill him with his usual optimism. He slogged around the edges of one, two, three little hills and emerged at a clearing. Here over ancient stumps and fallen branches and trunks the snow mounded up in bizarre shapes, hobgoblins, paplike mountains, castles of glass, sleeping dinosaurs. Fox scat. A lacework of busy paw prints in a land where the only living thing, it seemed, was feet.

And Jesse knew he was lost. Damned Canuck led him astray. He rested Grace against the ashbrown bark of a spruce. He paused to rest himself. Worn-out Hero. Aching back. His feet couldn't be colder if he were barefooted. They whined and whimpered. They wanted to be petted by warm hands. He couldn't do a thing about that. His boots were as good as welded on. Shoelaces fused with leather and leather fused with his skin. He'd need a blowtorch to get them off now. And he wished he had a blowtorch, too. He would put it to use on his girl first. Thaw her out a little. Then and only then would he attend to his own suffering doggies.

When he went to lift the girl up again she was like a ton of bricks. She was heavier than she'd ever been before. Put on weight somehow. He could barely manage her. Finally he got her over his shoulder, heaving all the way up from his feet. Her face looked at him coldly. He switched it to the other side. Now only her legs were looking at him. He staggered on an angle toward where he thought the road might be. Soon he was wobbling through a hollow filled with drifted snow. He came out of it and reached a rise and there shook himself from head to rear like a wet animal. Then he bent down and asked the Almighty kindly to make Grace well soon, very soon. He didn't know how much longer he could go on like this. As he straightened up he wondered could prayers work without a bed. He guessed not.

Sparse feathery snowflakes. Jesse clawing down the other side of the slope with his one free hand. Not long after that he hobbled into another clearing. Spruce swamp. Downy catkins with caps of snow. Stumps in the middle with thumbs up, brush coiled like chicken wire. And a low fog hanging over the ice like successive curtains of dingy cotton wool. You need a rest, he told the girl. He set her down and with a sigh fell backwards. World was nothing but grind, grind, grind. Just as in his granddad's time.

Reverie: Glimmery beach, and the men of Bravo Company resting on it with their shoes off. Bare feet dabbling in the warm sand. Some played poker, others cleaned their rifles, a few just bathed in the sun, brightest of all suns, the Vietnam sun. A couple of choppers floated lazily in the sky. Soldiers, shirtless, sat on their tanks. Everyone was smiling. They were waiting for the appearance of their new CO, who hailed from New Hampshire. From far down the beach came the cry: Here he comes! And he's draped in the flag! Immediately all the grunts scrambled to their feet and they cheered Hip! Hip! Hoorah! In the background someone was firing a twenty-one-gun salute . . . .

Crack! Crack! Crack!

The boy's salute was the ice breaking. Grace, doll-like and indifferent, had caved through its milky surface. He never should have set her down so close to the edge. *Swim!* he hollered, for a moment forgetting the girl was dead and couldn't swim. Her face was all he could see and then he couldn't even see that. Light though she was, she sank like a rock. Lampreys floated but she sank. Jesse didn't pause to ponder that mystery. He leaped up and flung himself in after her. Jolt of dreadful cold. The water was a knife cutting into his body. His plunge sent tremors through it and billowed Grace away from him. He churned the water frantically in an attempt to get to her. His churning drove her even farther away.

He came up sputtering. Sonofabitch! he screamed. His eyes tried to see through the murky depths.

This polar-bear plunge must have unsettled the boy's brain. As he looked around a stump sticking out of the water near him became Hack's bull face. He felt strong invisible hands pulling his legs down in the bottom muck. A rough voice said, Die you little queer! It occurred to him that Hack had come back to this world as a tree stump and now wanted to murder him. That would be just like Hack.

Jesse wasn't going to let himself go down without a fight. He still had so much to live for. He kicked at what held on to him. His arms whirled like propellers, he thrashed water and ice both with the fists of a fighter, Hero Jesse versus an entire swamp. His fright seemed to buoy him up. Then he realized he was standing in water that reached up only as far as his belly button. He shrugged and splashed his way onto dry land. Looking back he saw the stump was only a stump and not the enemy trucker. False alarm. But where Grace had been, he saw only black water around which flagstones of ice jammed and twirled. It was as though his girl had never been.

Jesse made quick little steps along the shore in

hopes of finding her. His wet jeans slapped his legs. He clumped through tussocks of grass and ran to the end of a spit of docked-up slash. There he tried to catch sight of an arm or a leg, any part of Grace. He stretched his eyes till they nearly burst their sockets. There was only debris. Ice drifting like a scum.

God kindly float her back to me I don't care if she's all stinky and dead she's mine oh kindly just a little breath to float her back . . . .

But God did not seem willing or able to salvage the girl. Jesse needed a bed to get his prayer safely across but beds don't grow on trees and around him there were only trees. He lurched back. You in there, Grace? he hollered out, though he hardly expected an answer. He knew the girl was gone by now. And he had let her go without even one last bit of loving. How he regretted that! How he wished he had pile-driven his cock into her one last time! Who could say that she wouldn't have felt it somewhere deep inside her lifeless body? His love was stronger than ice or swamp water.

Hands nearly leaping to his fly. The boy thought of Grace lying on her back in the ooze, dead spruce needles and snaky plants all around her. Frozen blue-faced girl. Limbs of wood. Good-looking despite all. He thought of her pussy, and in his mind it unfroze, thawed out like magic. Any blown-in-the-bottle pussy hound would howl at the sight of it. Her pink legs were parted wide enough to receive an army. And he was that army, was Jesse.

We gonna play your game again?

Uh-huh . . .

Oh goody. I always liked that little ole game.

Me too. My favorite game.

Love.

Love . . .

Well, soldier. What're you waiting for? Ram it home . . . .

I'm trying, Grace, the boy gasped. But try as he might, he could do nothing. Like putty, his nightcrawler. Soft and spineless. He tried slapping it but even that didn't help. At last he had to give up. The girl faded away, lost to his thoughts, lost in the deepening slime forever.

Perhaps it was the cold that did it. He was shivering. As he stood there with his cock in hand and none but the Almighty as his witness, wave after convulsive wave of cold swept over him. All the cold in the world, it seemed. His flesh fretted on his bones. His teeth chattered a mile a minute, saying nothing. The rest of him became mousetraps of ice clapping shut. Little bodies hopped on board. Skittering insect legs. Or were they infant rats crawling over him?

Some instinct deeper than love told Jesse to get his ass moving. The time had come to stop looking out for Grace and start looking out for himself. Or he'd become a tree like so many others before him. If he went on standing here like an idiot, the cold would surely be the death of him. He had to hit the road. Rouse his runner's legs and rouse them pronto. He had to reach Vietnam before he froze to death. No sense freezing to death.

So long, Grace, he said to the swamp. Someday I'll come back for you . . . .

And then he was careening through snowdrifts and snarls of brush again, tripping over buried logs, falling and picking himself up again. For nothing could keep this boy down now. Soon the old warmth returned to his body, and more. Prickles. They were swarming all over his skin. Prickles like tiny grains of sand stuck inside his underwear. He started to sweat. The sweat turned the prickles into sharp little sunbeams. It was not an unpleasant feeling at all.

Only once did Jesse stop and that was to zip up his fly, which happened to be undone.

Up ahead he thought he could see a group of soldiers playing catch. His platoon firing that horsehide back and forth. R & R. Waiting for their Jesse. It wouldn't be fair to burn any haythatch without him. I'm coming, guys, the boy hollered.

But up ahead never seemed to get there. The soldiers kept their distance. They seemed to back away as Jesse tottered toward them. They backed away but went on with their game of pepper. Did they think he had some sort of dread disease or what?

Yet the boy was able to see the occasional glimmer of jungle toward the back of his screen.

A grotesque forest creature coated with snow and running stifflegged. Something like a cross between an Abominable Snowman and a forlorn sniffling child. That was the sight Jesse presented. At first the game warden could not believe his eyes. He did a double take when he saw the boy come out of the woods with his arms waving wildly. Those arms pushed and shoved at him, pushed at his partner. The boy's face was twisted and fearful. He shouted: Get away get away from that water buffalo can't you see he's booby-trapped?

What the hell, kid?

You'll get blown to Kingdom Come!

Just a moose somebody cleaved the haunch off of . . .

The boy flung himself on the carcass to absorb the explosion. Defend his country. Save those poor grunts who couldn't save themselves. A Hero to the very end.

Hey Henry, he's that Boone kid. You know, the one they been looking for . . .

It was all the two of them could do to tear the boy away from the dead moose. They bundled him in a blanket where he sneezed and sniffled and uttered dire warnings about what would happen to them all. You got one heckuva bad cold, the warden told him.

Oughter get him to the police station, Henry . . .

Their snowmachine hauled the animal along to a nearby tote road and then they pulled the moose into the back of their truck. The boy was helped into the front. He sat huddled between the two men. Shivering. Head turned fearfully to look through the small window at the animal in back. Jesse couldn't believe it. You taking that buffalo along, too? he said. To him it was a madness. Like putting a lit bomb in your back pocket. Only a matter of time before it went off.

The warden turned to him. Kind weathered face. He said: That isn't a buffalo. You been watching too many cowboy movies. It's a moose and it's going to the Bethel Fish Hatchery. Grind it up there to make meal.

Don't look like no moose to me . . . .

Cow moose. Pregnant, too.

Preg . . . preg . . . preg?

Ayuh. Would have had a calf in about three weeks. But some fool hunter come along and killed it and cleaved off the hindquarters. Pretty serious offense up here. Five-hundred-dollar fine. Not many moose left in the north country. Guy who did that, why he should be shot . . . .

Jesse agreed whoever did it should be shot. He said he suspected Shanahan.

Shanahan? Shanahan? Don't know anyone by that name around here . . . .

Could the boy mean Jed Hanrahan, I wonder?

Not unless he killed that moose from his hospital bed. Jed's been in the Hitchcock for a month. Heart attack.

Guy should be shot, the boy said, yawning.

The warden: Now don't you worry about it, kid. We already retrieved the bullet. This afternoon we're going to seal off the area and get all the gun registrations. We'll find the guy, make no bones about it.

And Jesse didn't make any bones about it. He was asleep, his head lolling on the man's shoulder, rocking ever so slightly as the pickup went around bends.

Half in his slumberland the boy felt hands all around him. Hands that clasped his blanket tighter, hands leading him up steps. Soon he became aware that he was inside the Northton police station. He tried to pat his hair down, smooth it back. Very important to look nice for his friends the police. To the officer who asked him a few brief questions, he repeated what he'd told Officer Gagnon: Thanks for the bathroom.

More hands. A different blanket. Low voices and a glass of milk. At last his father arrived to take him away. The old man looked like he was getting ready to cry. Jesse, he said. We been looking all over for you. Where in God's name have you been?

Away, the boy said.

PART VI

Promised Land

New day, springlike, with a bright sun. That sun streamed through the windows of the old man's Plymouth but it stopped short of Jesse. He was shivering. He sneezed. He who never caught colds had caught a real humdinger. His head was filled with, he guessed, snot. He fisticuffed it but the snot stayed there. His hanky was already a wet rag. He switched to his sleeve.

Jesse reckoned he was going to Concord because of his cold. Sadly he sat in the back seat and blew his nose and listened as Jeff and his old man talked about poor Sam Pettigrew. Much of it was old hat to the boy. Sam was dead. He'd been found outside his trailer at the dump. The rats had been at him. What was left of the man wasn't a very pretty sight. One of the policemen had even thrown up while carting off the body. They were searching for Grace now. The old man said he couldn't believe it was the girl who did it.

You'll see, Jeff said. You'll see when they pick her up.

That little girl. She always looked so helpless to me.

Remember, it was the bullet that killed him. Any kid can shoot a .22.

I guess.

You know what Raymond said? He said they found her blood on the sheet.

Her blood?

Yeah. And he thinks Sam did to her what he done to Lucy and she shot him for it. Jeff cast an uneasy glance back at his brother as though maybe the boy shouldn't be hearing some of this. Certain squalid details might upset him.

Now isn't that a little farfetched, Jeff?

Girl was just defending herself. That's what Raymond says. He thinks old Sam had it coming to him.

But how could that scrawny little girl carry him all the way outside?

Adrenalin. Or maybe she didn't carry him out. Maybe he was already outside when she shot him.

Maybe she didn't shoot him at all, Jeff.

No one bothered to ask Jesse his opinion on the matter. He wouldn't have come out with that opinion anyway. He was hardly in the mood to shoot the shit. Subdued boy. With rheumy eyes he watched the towns pass by. Dingy little towns each with its own redbrick mill and boneyard. To him they all looked like Hollinsford. He figured that was why they all had signs with their names written on them. Signs on both sides of town. Just to be sure. So folks would know they weren't in Hollinsford.

Jeff went on talking to the old man. You believe every kid is a goody-two-shoes, he said. In Nam I seen girls Grace's age and younger do a whole lot worse. Come up to a guy and reach under his belt—you know?—and slip in a grenade . . .

Jesse's father donned his monkey face. He looked a thousand years old. He said: Hardly know what to believe anymore. First Hack. Now Sam. It's been a terrible week. And this trip doesn't make my heart rest any easier . . . .

I know. . . .

The two of them, both down there in the bug-
house, sighed the old man. Enough to make a person
wonder. Sometimes I think I'm next on the list, Jeff. . . .

Now don't say that. Everyone says you're doing
the right thing. Reverend. Ralph Perkins. Uncle Josh.
Everyone.

Jeff braked to avoid hitting a cat. They crossed an
old rickety bridge. The road curved into a highway
and they met with more traffic. Heading south now
they ended up behind a car with skis sticking out the
window. Mass. plates, Jeff said. Bet that guy won't be
back here till next winter.

Always hoped, the old man said. Hoped against
hope the boy would get better.

It wasn't your fault. You did everything you
could for him.

I wonder if I should have waited a little longer. . . .

Jeff said: Wait any longer and God only knows
what mischief he would have brewed up.

I don't think he means to be like that. . . .

It comes out trouble however he means it.

The poor boy . . .

By now Jesse had run out of sleeve space. His old
man turned around. You oughter blow your nose in
your hanky, son, he said.

Hanky's wetter'n my nose is. . . .

The old man handed him his own handkerchief.
He watched Jesse with sorrow in his eyes, like here
was one small joy—his son blowing his nose—that
he'd soon be without for the rest of his days.

For the longest time no one spoke. The land grew
gentler, the mountains fell away. They crossed another bridge, its steel struts in the shape of bold silver
X's. Jeff said: Concord's coming up. . . . Newer cars,
creeping traffic, more signs. They moved along an

endless lineup of hamburger stands, gas stations, and pizza palaces. A shopping plaza. Brick and glass plunked down into piles of blackish snow. It was a comfort to Jesse that Concord at least had a Miracle Mile.

Isn't it on Pleasant Street? Jeff asked.

Yeah. Turn right on New Boston Road.

Soon they turned. All the new buildings were gone. They drove down a street bordered by shabby clapboard houses. Some of those houses, Jesse thought, would feel right at home in the Hollow. They came to a gate and pulled up at a kiosk. It's a soldier, the boy whispered in awe. And the guard directed them to a small parking lot.

The old man said: If we admit him first, then they won't let us take him to see her.

Jesse reached for his brother's hand. Jeff shook him off. But his father took his hand, held it, leading him along.

Like visiting a plant, Jeff said. Year in and year out, she don't change. Beats me why you want him to see her.

I told you before. I want him to know about her. Kept it a secret for too long. I want him to know he's not alone here . . .

Christ he won't have to look far for company. . . .

. . . and it's better he found out from us instead of some nurse or orderly. That'd be a bad trick to play on the boy . . . letting one of them inform him. Bound to happen sooner or later.

I don't see what difference it makes who lowers the boom.

At least he'll have us right there beside him. In case it really upsets him. He's still your brother, Jeff.

Yeah. Brother Frankenstein.

They approached a fortresslike building. Gray stone upon gray stone. Battlements. The place had only a few windows and those were covered by bars. Once inside Jesse turned up his nose at the strong odor of disinfectant. At the desk his old man said: We're here to see Mrs. Boone. The woman nodded. Nurses scurried back and forth. To the boy they all looked like Mrs. Hack. Big white sponges. He almost giggled.

A nurse led them down a long corridor. An old woman in a wheelchair told them she had to go to the bathroom. Yells and laughter. A tray clattered to the floor and the boy had to sidestep a mush of corn and some other food green and unknown. . . .

They were in a large open room like a dormitory. Beds lined the walls. Jesse saw a woman trying to pull her hair out but not pulling hard enough. Another tapping her bedpan like it was a tambourine. Is this where I'm gonna be? the boy asked.

No, son. This is the women's section. We brought you here for a reason. We'd like you to meet someone very near and dear.

They stopped beside the bed of an old woman lying flat with her arms folded across her breast like she was dead. Wizened body in an old shapeless frock. Wilted nose, hair like wiremesh, spidery hands.

We brought you here to meet your mother. . . .

—*It's the witch!* Jesse hollered. His skin went cold.

The nurse propped up the woman. How you doing today? she said. You got visitors, dear.

Don't be afraid, boy. I should have told you about her long ago. Should have told you she was here. Couldn't. Too hard . . .

Jesse backed away, shaking his head. Nasty, he

hissed. That witch had come here after he'd given her the clout with the globe. She was recovering. Soon she'd rise up and haunt him again. He'd never be rid of her.

The old man took his arm and pushed him gently forward. Say hello to your mom. . . .

She's a nasty old witch, she's not my mom! My mom died. . . .

Oh Jesse, Jesse! How can I tell you? They said it was in her family. . . .

My mom went up the chimney . . .

They said she was too old. Came here after you were born. Just after it . . .

. . . up the chimney when I came down.

The old man moved to the side of the bed. Can you hear me, Betty? he said. This is your son here. Your son Jesse. See how big he's grown? The woman said nothing. She had a nibbling expression on her face like a sheep. And Jeff . . . you remember Jeff, don't you? The woman looked straight ahead without answering him.

See! Jesse shouted. She's no mom. . . .

She is, boy. She had this trouble. She was too old. She got very sad after you were born. Most women get that way but they get over it. Your mom, well, she . . .

She ain't no mom to me!

Please, son . . .

You came out of her same as I did, Jeff declared.

Out of *her*? The boy eyed that awful creature on the bed.

Jeff: Sure. You were once inside her. Right here. He made an extra big stomach with his hands.

No such thing! Jesse wailed.

Don't tell me you still buy that stork shit, Jeff said.

The boy ran toward the door. His father and brother started after him. He nearly knocked a legless woman out of her wheelchair. Crazy kids, she whimpered and weakly tried to hit him. But he was already out the door.

Where is he? the old man said, looking first one way, then the other.

They found him hunched basketlike on the hallway floor, his face cupped in his hands, sobbing. Never came out of no one, he cried, no one at all! An orderly was ready to attend him but Jesse's father waved the man away. He bent over the boy and stroked his hair and said, There now Jesse don't you cry. You're no different from other people. Everybody comes out of a mother.

No-o-o! the boy yelled. He flung his arms around his old man and held on for dear life. He buried his head in his old man's paunch. His father hugged him tight. It's going to be all right, son, he said, though his voice trembled like he felt nothing would ever be all right, ever again. You're a big boy now and big boys don't cry so wipe off those tears. . . . He took Jesse's hand again and helped him up and they headed out of the building.

So much for that idea, Jeff said.

Shouldn't have kept her a secret from him. That was my big mistake. He should have known.

You know what's a riot? He still believes in that stork and chimney stuff. After all these years . . .

They were walking very slowly now. The old man's face was wrinkled up in thought. He turned to Jeff as to an elder rather than a son. He said: Don't know if I'm doing the right thing by putting him here or not. . . .

Jeff sighed. Didn't Reverend say . . .

I know what Reverend said. But he's not Reverend's son. The boy is too young to be put away. I mean, if he was thirty, forty years old I probably wouldn't feel the same way about leaving him here. . . .

I thought we already decided on it. Geez, it's like we're back again to square one.

Every time I see your mother it just sets my mind to thinking. Don't want him to turn into a vegetable like her. I want the best for him. Oh Jeff I just don't know. . . . The poor little boy . . .

You know what he did to that Munson girl. Doesn't that convince you?

That was only once, Jeff. He may never rape anyone again.

I may never rape anyone again, Jesse repeated after his father.

They paused at the door of the admissions building. Feet of clay. The old man's grasp grew stronger. He held the boy back. They did not go in.